D1241117

THE RIVER OF FIRE

FRANÇOIS MAURIAC

THE RIVER
OF FIRE

(Le Fleuve de Feu)

Translated by

GERARD HOPKINS

LONDON
EYRE & SPOTTISWOODE

Le Fleuve de Feu *was originally published in Paris, 1923*
This first English translation was published in 1954

This book is made and printed in Great Britain
for Eyre & Spottiswoode (Publishers) Ltd., 15
Bedford Street, London, W.C.2, by Staples
Printers Limited, Rochester, Kent

If you wonder that a well-born young woman, and one not without piety, should fall as low as Gisèle de Plailly, then look into your own heart, which, no matter how devoted it may be to God, yet loves its own impurities still more.

For all that is in the world, the lust of the flesh, the lust of the eyes, and the pride of life, is not of the Father, but is of the world.

THE FIRST EPISTLE GENERAL
OF ST. JOHN: 2. 16

Unhappy that world which is burned rather than watered by these three rivers of fire, for it is accursed.

PASCAL

Oh God . . . who shall dare speak of this profound and shameful wound that nature bears, of the lust which binds the spirit to the flesh by bonds which are at once so tender and so violent?

BOSSUET

THE RIVER OF FIRE

I

D ANIEL TRASIS could see from his window that the paths were grass grown. He was the only person staying in this second class hotel. From the luxuriant flanks of the mountain came that animal smell which plantations of chestnut give off when the trees are in full leaf. From beneath the hooves of a flock of sheep in motion, dust, reeking of greasy fleeces, rose into the air. He heard the hotel omnibus setting off for the station with much rattling of windows, grinding of brakes, and tinkling of bells. "If it comes back empty, I shall stay on: if it brings other visitors, I shall return to Paris." In this way did the young man try to persuade himself that the prospect of solitude held no threat. A sudden, heavy shower swept across the sun, lashing the leaves, and then passed on in a diminishing patter of drops. The cheep of birds sounded sharper. Never had Daniel Trasis been so completely alone. He closed his eyes and conjured up a vision of this late afternoon as it must be in Paris, with all its various sights and smells – the early summer rain reviving the leaves on the trees in the Avenue Henri Martin, giving to the trunks a new washed look, and to the macadam of the roadway a sur-face of shining black. This time, a year ago, Thérèse Her-

lant had just left him. He had been so miserable, so in-
tolerably strung up, that the only way he could escape
from his obsession was by getting Raymond Courrège
to take him every day for a run in the Hispano. At night-
time, looking like a couple of masked bandits, the friends
had roared their way along the empty streets. Paris, deserted and sweet smelling, seemed to contract beneath
their wheels. They flew across its diminished distances.
How short a stretch between the Concorde and the Point
du Jour! They stopped at bars, and, in the dawn light,
drank bowls of early-morning soup in the Markets. And
now, here he was, seeking safety from that same Thérèse
Herlant in a Pyreneean valley – no longer jealous to be
sure, but with his nerves on edge, and dreading nothing
so much as the hot and desperate pursuit of an ageing
woman. Leaving her husband and children, with some
trumped up excuse, at Blois, she had taken to turning up
unheralded – not to ring his doorbell, for she knew that
he was never now at home to her – but to stand concealed behind one of the trees of the Avenue, all eyes for
his appearance. "You're weak!" – that had been Raymond's verdict: "a damn good hiding, that's what she
needs, and if it was me, she wouldn't have long to wait!
. . ." But Daniel had preferred to run away.

"I've got to stick it out for another fortnight – two
weeks and no more" – he told himself. Nothing humili-

ated him so much as failing to carry out a plan he had made, and it had been his intention to stay for a month in this dead-and-alive health resort. Why hadn't he remained in the city, and just hidden from Thérèse? A criminal on the run always finds it best to cling to densely populated centres. He dreamed of the broken-springed divan in Raymond Courrège's little hallway. Many a good night had he spent there – gone to ground, hidden beyond finding, inaccessible, anonymous, delivered from the pressure of his fellows, while, on the other side of the wall Raymond was busy tumbling some girl or other until sleep overcame them both, and all sounds merged into a calm breathing, into the nocturnal innocence of a children's nursery. On those occasions Daniel would lie on his back watching beneath the door the gleam of the staircase light when one of the tenants came in late. Above his head was a shelf laden with hatboxes, old shoes and suitcases. Someone, somewhere, would rattle a key, slam a door, and darkness would once more descend upon the stairs. The dawn chorus of innumerable birds would reach him from the walls of a narrow garden, and later, waking out of a delicious slumber, he would hear the faint clink of milk bottles being set down on the landing, and the rustle of newspapers and letters being pushed under the door.

"If the bus comes back empty, I stay on." The train

must have been late." Daniel's idle gaze came to rest upon
the bedside table where stood the only photograph that
never left him. It was a portrait, not of his parents, but
of his uncle Louprat, who lived at la Sesque, and had left
him the modest independence which he now enjoyed.
At Bourrideys, in the room with the north-west aspect,
his father had killed himself. The kindlier neighbours had
explained the deed by his despair at the thought of having
to outlive his wife. But others there were who remembered that his vines had suffered badly from the hail that
year. The older ones among them recalled that Monsieur
Trasis, the "old man of Sesques", had dragged out a peasant existence in the Château of la Sesque beyond the
Sauterne country, a house stuffed with pigeons, blood-
spattered hares, woodcock and cornfed chickens. He
had hanged himself in the storeroom, surrounded by
padlocked racks where, in dusty bottles, there lingered
on the summer warmth of the century's first years. Daniel
had loved, as a boy, to give his feelings play, to frighten
himself and sob his heart out in front of the fireplace in
that north-west room, where once, as he knew, the floor
had quivered beneath the weight of a falling body. Later,
when he read in his manual of philosophy, that suicide is
quite often an inherited tendency, the memory became
with him a tormenting obsession. Of this he had been
cured in time, but he had never forgiven his father, and

thought of him with a sense of bitter grievance, which extended to the whole of his family – the relations living at Bazas, those at Captieux, his aunt at Sore, his cousins at Landirats. But for Louprat of la Sesque, his guardian and his grand-uncle, he had retained a fellow feeling. He had a sort of cult for the old man, and would pore over his portrait in the family album. The picture at which he thus gazed showed a sly old face perched on a high collar, and thumbs stuck into waistcoat pockets; the likeness of a man who had read all the novels of Paul de Kock as he journeyed between Langon and Bordeaux in some of the earliest trains to run in that part of the country. He had spent so much money on improving the château of la Sesque, that he had finally ruined himself, and, some time after '70, on the advice of his friend Jérome David, had sold the estate, being persuaded that the Emperor and Empress would use it as a stopping place when the Court moved from Paris to Biarritz. He had ended his days in a house on the tree darkened Square of the market town adjoining Bourrideys. He believed in God and hated priests. In October, 1915, he had breathed his last in an equivocal ground floor flat in the rue des Remparts at Bordeaux.

When the omnibus returned Daniel noticed on its roof a trunk and travelling bag. He sighed happily: "This means that I clear out!" The Pédebidous, who owned the hotel, hastened out, on the heels of the porter, to the front steps. In the light of the setting sun Daniel caught sight of Monsieur Pédebidou's bald head, of Madame Pedebidou's curls and short arms, to which the pressure of her stays gave the appearance of an insect's wing cases, and of Mademoiselle Pédebidou's bony shoulders and lank hair. Only the arrival of a guest could thus marshal the full force of this family, the members of which were, as a rule, visible only behind the frosted glass of the office. A young lady got out of the omnibus. She was young, and wore a toque with a veil. Daniel repeated to himself – "I'm off tomorrow". He heard a confused babble of voices above which that of the newcomer was clearly audible.

"Hasn't Madame de Villeron arrived?" She repeated her question, with additions: "A lady with one small daughter? . . . " and, when the Pédebidous called one another to witness that no letter had been received . . . "I can't understand it. My friend had arranged for us to meet here this evening."

What seemed to surprise her more than anything else was that no telegram had come for her. But Madame Pédebidou, as though she were in receipt of some mysterious information, promised the lady of the omnibus that she would certainly have a telegram next morning: "the very first thing, Madame: you can set your mind at rest on that score."

The voices faded away across the entrance hall, then rose again as the group mounted the stairs. A nearby door creaked. Daniel Trasis changed into a short jacket and black tie, shaved carefully, and, on the second stroke of the dinner gong, came down and walked across the hall to where the "List of Arrivals" was displayed. Until today his had been the only name upon it, but already another had been written beneath it – Mademoiselle de Plailly. A young girl, then? He quite understood why the absence of her friend had upset her, since not for a moment did he doubt that she must be very young. Almost certainly, in order to facilitate the routine of dinner, their tables would be set side by side in the restaurant, and it was with a feeling of acute disappointment that he found himself once again dining alone, with nothing to break the silence but the creaking of the high-capped, gaunt old serving woman's new boots. She informed him that the young lady was taking dinner in her room – though with nothing to speak of in the way of appetite: "All in a dither, she is, the poor dear." Daniel ordered a half bottle of Cliquot. He no longer felt bored. He had often compared himself to a rat whose teeth must never remain inactive for a single moment. He went out on to the road to await the coming of darkness, responsive less to the rustlings and the smells which reminded him of the June nights of his childhood under a familiar sky,

B

than to what was peculiar to this Pyreneean valley, with
its high-set plateau still touched by the sinking sun and
noisy with the sound of the cracked bells of browsing
sheep and of the little chapels which he could not see.
There was a drifting mist breaking into eddies at the level
of the quiet grass. But of more than all else, he was conscious of the rushing mountain torrents, of that indeter-
minate sound of living waters which brings, when evening comes, to every little valley of the Pyrenees, a super-
natural sweetness, a lulling whisper of eternity – as though
intent on bringing to the human spirit a foretaste of that
Peace and Refreshment promised by the liturgy of the
Church.

Mademoiselle de Plailly, a young girl. . . . There are
few men who do not cherish some secret longing. For
Trasis a hunger and thirst after the innocence of youth
had long been an obsession. For all his profligate self-
indulgence he knew that he was powerless in the presence
of untouched simplicity, and the knowledge humiliated
him. He had never admitted this weakness to any of his
friends. It was in vain that Raymond Courrège assured
him that dancing, since the war, had vastly enlarged the
possibilities of sex. Daniel, because he had been wounded
in the left foot at Vauquois, avoided dancing like the
plague. "You're quite wrong", Raymond would say:
"the only difference, when a chap's lame is that the girls

take a bit longer to make up their minds. They may seem
to be a bit put off at first, but they always come back in
the long run, especially the ones who have been most put
off . . . " His own especial pleasure was to break his women
in and force them to comply with his amorous fantasies.
Daniel pretended to be afraid of intrigues with young
girls, and of their possible consequences, even though
Raymond assured him that the modern young thing was
fully informed about the ways in which motherhood
might be avoided. When he spoke like that, however,
Daniel would shake his head without answering, and as he
never spoke about his secret cravings, Raymond made a
great joke of his friend's jealous frenzies, which led him
to scrutinize the past of each of his mistresses (he had lived
in a state of martyrdom for several weeks because of
something that Thérèse Herlant had told him about a
young man she had known at Cabourg, when she was a
girl, and of how she had "got a thrill" from watching
him go in to bathe). What women loved in him was that
for all his pleasant sunburned face and dreamy eyes, there
was something of the brute in him – which no doubt,
was the direct result of his particular mania. "It's because"
he said, "they've already been through the hoop, and
show dirty finger marks."

It was of Mademoiselle de Plailly that he was thinking
as he wandered along the country road where the homing

cows forced him against the parapet. He summoned from
his past the memory of the girl who, beyond all doubt,
had given him this longing for simplicity. The country
town of Bazardais, where, in the old days, Uncle Louprat
had entertained him during the holidays, had held few
attractions for a schoolboy. It was beyond his comprehension that his uncle, living, as he did, all the year round
in the country, should enjoy the fact that his windows
gave directly on the Square with its dark, overshadowing,
and enormous planes, and that his backyard should be
forever filled with the screeching of a nearby sawmill.
It was enough for Uncle Louprat to know that he possessed a quantity of "standing timber". So great was his
pride that he would rather have seen his trees rot where
they stood than have them felled. Ever since the sale of
la Sesque – which the Emperor, after all, had never visit-
ed – he had lived in constant dread of being thought to
be in want of money. Concealed in the ground floor
"office", with its chocolate coloured panelling, he spent
the days watching the comings and goings of his neighbours, and especially of the Curé, of whose visits to the
ladies in the post-office he would keep a careful tally, and
about which he would make endless sly jokes. In this way
he took his revenge for something that the priest has said
to the children of Mary to the effect that "any girl who
took a place as servant with Louprat was lost". There was

in his room a cupboard which contained, in addition to a bottle of very old brandy, a number of laboriously obscene Japanese prints. Casanova, Restif de la Bretonne, and the Marquis de Sade, contributed to his delight. In the corner reserved for the philosophers, he had assembled Voltaire's *Facéties*, the *Testament du Curé Meslier*, the *Alcoran des Cordeliers*, the *Jésuites criminels*, a *History of the Flagellants*. It was only after the old octogenarian's somewhat ambiguous death that his nephew had discovered the hidden hoard with the help of which he had secretly fanned his dwindling fires. During those holidays of his adolescent years, the boy's only pleasure had been to bicycle the five miles which separated him from Bourrideys, where his father had killed himself – a village so remote and hidden that the road stopped at it and went no further. In August, the caretakers, mother and father Ransinangue, and their daughter Marie, would fling wide the windows of the house to let in the sun, though nothing they could do ever succeeded in getting rid of its mouldy smell. Four rows of enormous oaks, low-branched and tangled, lay between it and a field of blighted maize. It was in this wilderness of earth and sky, circled by gloomy pines, that the young Daniel, and the still younger Marie Ransinangue, saw animals and chariots and gods in the drifting clouds.

Marie Ransinangue had taken her school certificate

well before the usual age. According to the head-mistress, Sister Lodois, she was a remarkable child. Each day she would walk ten miles, simply in order to *learn*. "Everything goes into that little head", said the good sister, and painted for the girl's benefit a bright picture of the glories and delights of the novitiate. The strong, firm curves of the young fifteen-year-old in her country smock had produced in Daniel Trasis a species of delicious torment. Even now, after all the debauch and easy pleasure which Paris had brought him, those distant feelings flooded back at the mere sight of a strange young woman's name – Mademoiselle de Plailly.

The road lay empty before him. In his ears was the plashing of the mountain torrent. The sound of his footsteps interrupted the singing of a nightingale. "Marie Ransinangue" he said, "Marie Ransinangue". Such pleasure had her artlessness given him that though, when he met her first, he had already lost his innocence, he abstained from making any attempt to corrupt her. She was a pious little thing, to be sure, but full, too, of gaiety and laughter. Nothing about her led him to suppose that she had lent a willing ear to the suggestions of Sister Lodois. She took delight in running after him through the empty house, in decking herself out in odds and ends of old clothes from the garret, in lying on the grass at the edge of the great meadow and reading aloud from the

novels of Maryane, Raoul de Navery, and Zénaïde
Fleuriot, books from which Sister Lodois had derived
her knowledge of the world and human passions, and
might, she thought, be safely entrusted to the girl for her
enjoyment. There was never, between the two of them,
anything but childish prattle, into which mother Ransinangue would break when it was time for Marie to
busy herself about the poultry and the pig. The pretty
creature was innocent of sentimental moodiness. The
most she ever did by way of dalliance was to sit staring
at Daniel until he told her to "take that moon-calf look
off her face". One August day, on her way back from
Vespers – it was the fifteenth of the month, and therefore
a holiday occasion – dressed absurdly in her festival gar-
ments, she had said: "I communicated for you this morning." Hearing this he had burst out laughing, so that she
looked at him with her brows drawn together in a frown,
while he had eyes for nothing but her muslin – swathed
and whaleboned body sweating in the heat. After a pause,
he said with an expression that was not quite like his usual,
untroubled look – "You must have been hot, Marie," at
which she gave a foolish grin and ran off to catch up with
her mother. From that day, though no words passed between them, she took to avoiding him. He looked else-
where for his pleasures, but knew that Marie was teaching
the urchins of Bourrideys their catechism, decking the

hair of brides and First Communicants – after first rid-
ding them of their lice – and watching by the dead. Then
he forgot Marie Ransinangue entirely. He never so much
as heard her name until he came home on his first leave
in the war years. On that occasion, Uncle Louprat had
made a lot of sneering remarks about the hysterical wave
of mysticism which had been sweeping the district ever
since mobilization, telling him how a young shepherd lad
had been hearing voices, and that one of the farmers'
wives had had visions, and claimed to be able to say defi-
nitely that so-and-so who had been posted as "missing"
was alive and well.

"You'll never guess what that little Ransinangue girl
has done! Why, just to show how devoted she is to the
family, she's vowed to go into a nunnery if you come
back safe and sound!"

Daniel, at that, had smiled and shrugged. But some
time later, at Monsieur Louprat de la Sesque's funeral
service, to be precise (all solemn pomp and piety, for the
old gentleman had never tired of saying to the Curé,
"nothing doing so long as I'm alive and kicking, but you
can have me when I'm dead") while the offertory bag was
going round, he was conscious of Marie's eyes fixed upon
him. Her stare was quite unabashed. It was as though she
knew that this was the last time she would ever look at
him, since, either he would be killed, or, if he did return,

she would bury herself alive. And so it was that, in the last days of 1918, the girl vanished from the world. It was known that she had entered the Carmelite House at Toulouse. When, after demobilization, he came back to Bourrideys to see how much resin had been tapped from his trees, and to check the accounts, he realized from the air of dumb resentment with which the Ransinangues met him, that they held him to be responsible for the sorrow that had fallen upon them. But by that time he was too wholly obsessed by the pleasure of being alive, in doing deals, as Raymond Courrège's partner, in cars and motorcycles, electric-light bulbs, aeroplane fabric, American uniforms, and tinned food, and in leading a life of profligacy, to spare a thought for the reclusion of his childhood's friend – or persuaded himself that he was. But sometimes, on Raymond's divan, at dance halls, or in the Hispano on a Sunday, when they drove out to some suburban hotel with a cargo of girls, he would have a momentary vision of his little country companion on her knees. With extraordinary clarity he would see a red-tiled floor, a pitcher full of water, a whitewashed wall, and a crucifix.

And now, this evening, on the darkening road, filled for a moment with a lively company of singing boys and girls, his thoughts were all of Marie Ransinangue.

One lighted window broke the dark mass of the hotel.

As he crossed the hall, he shot a furtive glance at the delicious name – *Mademoiselle de Plailly*, and decided that he would stay on for two more days.

Next morning he saw her at the Reception Desk. Her hair was hidden under a simple straw hat, but it must, he guessed, from the freckled paleness of her childish cheeks, be red. He noticed the firm column of her neck, the cropped curls showing under the back of the hat. For that sort of hair he had a peculiar weakness. She was turned side-face to him, and was deep in a lively discussion with Madame Pédebidou who, uncomfortably conscious of her dressing-gown and curlers, was speaking through the half-closed door of the Office. No doubt about it, she was young – but just at that too brief moment of flowering womanhood which warns the potential lover how short a time remains for conquest. Any day now, the lovely fruit might be handled and bruised. He lurked in the shadows, feasting his eyes on the still undamaged prey. She was holding an open telegram in her hand, and was issuing instructions in a firm, decided tone.

"Madame de Villeron will be here this evening – the child's not been very well . . . Please get the room next to mine ready – the one with the communicating door . . . Not such a good outlook? – well, that doesn't matter . . . Madame de Villeron would rather have a communi-

cating door than a fine view . . . and don't forget a bed
for the child . . . a cot? – oh, dear me, no: the little girl is
four, and big for her age."

She turned away and went out of the front door. A
threatening cloud, hidden until now by the mountain,
had suddenly taken the colour from the sky. The sun
went in, leaving the heavily fluttering butterflies to look
for it in the grass. Daniel sauntered along the road, thinking of nothing but the offered prey. He was in a mood
of mingled anger and delight, the pain and pleasure so
mixed in him that, at present, he could not separate the
two emotions. There was plenty now for the rat to use
his teeth on. He was brought up short by the idea of "this
Villeron woman" – for so his nascent hatred had already
named the prospective arrival. Who was the friend whom
the girl seemed so impatient to have with her? There was,
at least, some comfort in the knowledge that she was a
mother. But why this assignation a good four hundred
miles from Paris? How oppressive the sunless heat was!
The buzzing of innumerable insects rose from the exhausted earth. By way of a mountain path he reached a
tumble-down and seemingly abandoned village. He would
have thought it empty of all life but for the fact that
when he went into the church he found the Sanctuary
lamp alight. The sudden coolness struck sweetly on his
face, his eyes, his hands. On the vaulted ceiling were

paintings of birds and flowers. The altar lilies, imprisoned since the previous day, filled the shadowed interior with a thick and heavy scent. Gradually, as his eyes grew accustomed to the darkness, he noticed the humble furniture of faith – the bier for funerals, the book of antiphons standing on a desk which was greasy with candle droppings. His mind went back to his schooldays when he had been in the habit of taking into chapel a provision of profane reading disguised between the covers of a prayer-book. Uncle Louprat's waggish jokes, culled from Léo Taxil's "Comic Bible", and the songs of Béranger about Curés and their housekeepers, had set him against religion, though less, probably, than the staggering discovery, on the occasion of his First Communion, that he had felt nothing more thrilling than the demands of an empty stomach. But, during his year in the top classical form, he had, for a while, come under the influence of the weakliest of all his school companions, Jean Péloueyre, the "hobbledehoy", as he was called, of whose repressed and unspoken affection he was fully aware, and from whom he acquired a taste for continually repeating lines of poetry. Can we ever wholly escape from the influence of those who feel for us a deep and burning love? Those who love us leave on our characters a more lasting mark than those we love. At that period of his life, Daniel, an over-grown, over-sensitive, and coarse lout of a boy,

had learned to read not only all the poets, but Epictetus
and the Gospel into the bargain. He came to entertain for
Uncle Louprat feelings of contempt, almost of hatred,
when after dinner on August evenings, he watched him
pour out a glass of Gruau-Larose with a hand which shook
so violently that half the wine was spilled upon the cloth
("takes his red wine, he does, at every meal, and has done
for these last sixty years" – said Ransinangue with awed
admiration). Sometimes the old man would try to draw
Daniel out, asking him questions which the boy eluded.
He took him to the Grand Theatre in Bordeaux, and
pinched his arm during the ballet, with a whispered –
"take a good squint at the Lovati – last on the left – catch
hold of the glasses".

Thus dreaming, and thus remembering, Daniel sat on
in the little lost church. So forgetful was he of the time,
that, suddenly conscious of his hunger, he had to hurry
back to the hotel and go straight to the dining-room
without waiting to wash his hands. As he opened the
door, Mademoiselle de Plailly turned her head for a moment and looked at him. He felt a momentary shock of
annoyance that she should see him thus all flushed and
unkempt. But it passed almost immediately. Raymond
Courrège always said – "You're the type they prefer in
the raw." He was surprised that she did not repeat the
movement, and then grew uneasy as he realized that the

mirrors were so arranged as to make it possible for her to fix him with her eyes without appearing to do so. However, the realization that she was playing this little trick gave him a pleasurable thrill. But there was something of pain in the pleasure. Until she had finished her strawberries, the fair unknown continued with her elaborate pretence of not being aware of his presence. But he was not taken in. He knew, only too well, that particular manoeuvre which consists of seeming to look at anything and anyone but the face one wants to study. He, for his part, had a far from clear view of her. He was short-sighted, but would not, for any consideration in the world, have spoiled his appearance by wearing spectacles, or make himself ridiculous by sporting a monocle. The girl's hair, caught in a ray of sunlight, showed as less red than he had expected. He would have found it hard to describe in words the dark, flamelike quality of its colouring. He began to make excuses for her: "she can't see that I see what she's up to," he thought: but would have given a good deal if she would only stop staring at his reflection. She took a swerving course to the door like a wounded partridge.

He spent the rest of the day in aimless wandering, though never going far from the hotel, and his constant thought was – "the Villeron woman will be here this evening. I must wait and see what she's like".

When the hour of the train's arrival drew near, she crossed the hall in full flight towards her friend. She half opened the door of the Office and asked an invisible Pédebidou to see that two vases, deep enough to hold long-stemmed flowers, were put in Madame de Villeron's room. This delicate attention irritated Daniel. He took up a commanding position in the hall from which he would be able to get a good view of the unknown enemy. It looked as though the train had been late. The postman arrived with a telegram which he handed to Madame Pédebidou. Daniel heard the muttered name of Mademoiselle de Plailly, and so great was his joy that he could stay still no longer, but got up from his chair and started to walk up and down. He felt convinced that the Villeron woman was announcing a further delay, and began to take stock of the influence he might exercise over the solitary prey. Then he went to earth again.

Sure enough, when the 'bus drew up at the door, Mademoiselle de Plailly got out of it alone. The misery showing in her face filled him with a frenzy of exasperation. She opened and read the telegram: she voiced her disappointment. "The child's gone and developed croup, now! – that's what she says here: mild attack croup. Impossible come at present. Letter follows . . ." Madame Pédebidou hastened to reassure her . . . since it wasn't serious her friend would certainly turn up within the week . . . The young woman, not seeing Daniel, came to a dead stop in the middle of the hall. "I don't know *what* I ought to do", she said in a low voice, then went and sat down on a bench just outside the door. Daniel sauntered across. He could make, through the glazed panel, a leisurely examination of her shoulders and the back of her neck as though studying them through a magnifying glass. What a fool he had been to neglect such an opportunity! He made his way towards her, and noticed that she was crying. At his approach she raised her head. The wind, as though in league with him, blew the telegram from her lap. He picked it up, gave it back to her, and ventured on a few words. He knew, he said, from the Pédebidous that she had had bad news. If there was anything he could do for her, she had only to say. At this suggestion she took no offence, but answered as a woman who had missed a train might have spoken to a porter who had offered her his help. So eager was she for advice that she poured the most priceless items of information into his attentive ears. Did he think she'd better go home? Travelling was such an expensive business nowadays! Her father lived in one of the Paris suburbs and certainly would not fork out a second time just so as she could go and see her friend in Dunkirk. The opportunity for a meeting would be lost. On the other hand, ought she to stay on here alone for a week, or perhaps longer? There was the hotel bill to be considered . . . though of course her friend would look after that . . .

"Does she do the paying?"

"Oh, she's a great deal better off than I am . . ."

She broke off, her cheeks ablaze, overcome by the embarrassment of having given herself away. He dared not look at her while, with feigned indifference, he said that if she'd take his advice she would wait until the promised letter came before making up her mind. She got up from her seat with murmured apologies and thanks.

Daniel walked quickly down the road as though somebody were waiting for him. It was his way of coming to terms with himself when opposed feelings had him in their grasp, desire and fear, anguish and joy . . . He knew that on one point his mind was made up. He would stay on. But not for the life of him could he have said which of the many conflicting emotions in his heart was dominant – disappointment at not, so far, having made the acquaintance of the Villeron woman – hope of the kind that always seized on him whenever a young and defenceless creature, already lightly wounded, came within range of his gun – happiness at being alone to pursue the intrigue on which he had decided to embark, without any witness to embarrass him, and especially not Raymond Courrège. Had *that* hard task-master been present, he almost certainly, from a false sense of shame, would have

c

taken by assault the gentle prey which had no thought to flee from him. Now, probably for the first time, he could follow the dictates of his own nature. Of nothing was he more certain than of his desire to ravish the offered flesh, of nothing, except possibly of his fear that it might, after all, be not untouched already. He would have given anything to know that she was still innocent of the traffic of sex. What he most longed for was that she should have been till now, another Marie Ransinangue kept in a cloister from the eyes of men. Was it jealousy that worried him? He knew that his present passion went far beyond jealousy as ordinarily understood, for when in imagination – and his imagination was quick to act, and patient in the attainment of its ends – he tried mentally, to strip and to possess her, he suffered almost as much from that fantasy of passion as he would have done from seeing her delivered to another.

At dinner that evening she gave him a brief nod of recognition, after which she never looked once at him, even furtively. This relapse into her former attitude of indifference did not worry him. He would let her run free, would give her the illusion of liberty, for he was strong in the knowledge that he could pounce on her at will and take his pleasure when he would. He was in no hurry. During the progress of the meal he even found himself wishing that the enemy, the Villeron woman,

were there. It would have pleased him to do open battle
with her. How sad her absence seemed to make the girl,
who sat with her elbows on the table, a brooding look
in her eyes, and her guard lowered. She had not changed
out of the dusty skirt and the blouse which she had been
wearing that afternoon.

Dinner over, he went out into the garden. It was strident with the grating of cicadas, and the heat of the day
hung stagnant beneath the chestnuts. He tried to answer
a question that was gnawing at him – "why should I soil
her? . . ." After some moments he lit a cigarette, not
knowing that the young girl was watching from the terrace the brief flare of the match between his cupped
hands. At that very moment he was repeating the question to himself – "why soil her? – why even think of
doing such a thing? . . ." How Raymond would laugh if
he could hear him now! "What d'you mean by soil",
he'd say . . . "acts are the only thing that matter in life,
and one act's as good as another . . ." What was it he
wanted of this girl? Would her body, after hours and
hours of pleasure, be any different from what it was now
in its virgin state? "What I see in her is nothing but a
mirage. Purity? – what *is* purity? . . ."

The thick foliage above his head was rustling. The
whole countryside seemed filled with the sound of living
waters beneath a moonless sky swarming with little points

of light, crossed by a milky way, a pale waterfall of radiance. This ceaseless murmuring of streams in earth and sky, gave him a feeling that every stain might be removed, and cleanliness restored, by water.

After midnight there came a momentary whisper of falling rain, and when the dawn broke it was pattering still upon the leaves and all the happy birds. The mountain was no longer visible. The myriad-meshed network of the rain kept Daniel and Mademoiselle de Plailly prisoners within the hotel. When, in the dining-room, he asked her whether better news had reached her, she answered briefly that her friend would be arriving at the end of the following week, and made it quite clear that she did not wish to prolong the conversation. He bowed, and blessed her silently for being on the defensive. He liked her to be distrustful. From where he stood on the terrace, he could see through the glazed door of the hotel drawing-room, that she was busy writing an interminable letter – no doubt her answer to the Villeron woman. It hurt him that she should find it possible to cover so many pages. Not for anything in the world would he leave his point of vantage until she had finished. To give himself a pretext for remaining where he was, he took out the letter which he had received that morning from Raymond Courrège, and read it through again. It was dated from a bar in the Champs-Elysées and on the second page there was the brown burn of a cigarette. Raymond had nothing to complain of so far as business was concerned. He had netted a cool 5,000 on a Voisin which he had bought and sold again all within forty-eight hours. He couldn't use the Hispano any longer, having stuffed it full of silk samples, and he'd brought off a wonderful deal. No sooner had he touched his commission than along had come a bloke with an offer of a job lot of stuff at rock bottom price. He was hoping to make a good thing out of that – and he jolly well needed to, with champagne the price it was at *El Garone* and the *Acacias*. He'd got rid of Marcelle but picked up a little peach of an Argentine – a mere schoolgirl of eighteen. Nothing of the tart about *her*! The first time she'd been to see him, he'd treated her to some of his famous mulled wine and cinnamon.

Daniel tore the letter into little pieces, staring all the while through the glazed door at Mademoiselle de Plailly still at her endless writing . . . Though he had destroyed Raymond's letter, the sight of that brown burn had roused, in some odd way, the more bestial part of his nature. The girl in the room was now no more to him than she would have been to a womanizer like Courrège. Ah, if he could only force the lock of the door, tear from her hands the sheets and sheets of paper on which she had been inscribing her most secret thoughts, and possess her

here and now, forcing her to submit to his will! Just as
she rose to her feet, and stood for a moment licking the
envelope, he entered the room and stayed by the door
staring at her. He was against the light, and the rain had
filled the room with dusk. She could not, therefore, see
the atrocious expression of his face. But she must have
felt a hint of danger in the air, for she hurried into the
hall. Daniel remained where he was, gazing at the crochet
antimacassars on the rosewood chairs, at the wild goat's
head over the door, at the table where, a moment before,
she had been writing. There was a sheet of blotting paper
on it. This he greedily seized and proceeded to examine in
front of a looking-glass. He managed to make out a few
unimportant words . . . love . . . kisses . . . rain . . . and
the signature: Gisèle de Plailly. He carried the memory
of that Christian name away with him, repeating it to
himself, savouring its sweetness, letting it sink deep into
his consciousness. It brought him peace: it calmed him.
Standing at the window of his bedroom, smoking, dreaming, looking at the rain, and drinking in something of
the joy of the drenched leaves, he played with each syl-
lable of the two names: Gisèle – Gisèle de Plailly – as
though they had been a charm with which to open unknown doors.

When rain falls in the Pyrenees it lasts for a long time.
Three days passed without a break in the deluge which

blotted out the mountains and contracted the visible world to a small space round the deserted hotel. The rain was in league with his desires. It would hand her over, abandoned, bound hand and foot, to do with as he would. Not that he was so fatuous as to ignore the possibility that she might find him unattractive; but he trusted to his instinct to tell whether the way ahead was open, whether he could take his chance. It was one of his strong points that he could see himself without illusion, as the woman of his choice might see him. It was as though, in spite of himself, he must conform to his image in her eyes, must play the part of enemy for which she had cast him. One word, one look, had often sufficed to make him feel vulgar, even trivial. On the other hand, his flesh was quickly roused to awareness at the smallest sign of response. The least indication of surrender found in him a ready recipient. And so it was that he felt convinced that he could take Gisèle by storm. He delighted in her wariness like a "gun" who revels in the manoeuvres of the game bird which is fated to fall to him. No need for pursuit. Later he was to remember, as the only peaceful moments of his love, these hours in the empty hotel, the sound of the imprisoning rain, the tip-tap of furtive footsteps on the terrace, while he sat in the drawing-room turning the pages of an old bound volume of *Le Monde Illustré*, and, above all, the face of the young girl, gone

suddenly blank, when, at mealtimes he stole a quick
look at the mirror in which he knew that the eyes of the
beloved were watching him. He was of those whom a
woman has the power to wound from the first moment
of words exchanged.

When newcomers arrive at an hotel their sudden presence has a way of creating a sort of intimacy among those
already there. A day came when a strange family was
seen filing into the dining-room: first, an elderly woman
squeezed into a tight pair of stays which showed a ridge
across her back, then an enormously tall, half-starved-
looking son, whose Adam's apple, moving ceaselessly up
and down, looking like the mark of some obscure disease,
and a pimply face. Last of all came the father with the
majestic carriage of a farmyard fowl. He had a bald and
scarlet head supported on a high stiff collar, and, with
his drooping, veined, and fleshy dewlaps produced the
impression of a turkey. Daniel and Gisèle glanced at one
another, smiled. It was she who, in the drawing-room,
before he had even asked her for her news, told him that
the child was making a "rather slow recovery", but that
her friend hoped to be with her before the week was out.
She added:

"You'll never guess what Madame Pédebidou says is
wrong with that gawky youth. It appears that his heart

is too small for his body, with the result that the blood never reaches his extremities!"

In that case, they agreed, his hands and feet must be blue with cold. The shared joke made them feel like friends of long standing. They were amazed. It was as though the few days during which, without a word spoken, they had never ceased to think of one another, had brought them closer together than any amount of revealing talk could have done. They wondered at the progress they had made. She announced the receipt of a letter by quoting what Maeterlinck had said about hearts knowing one another without employing the medium of bodies. He, rather daringly, replied that it was bodies, not hearts, that reacted at a distance, each sniffing the scent of the other, and feeling the magnetism of attraction. . . . At this she burst into a really horrible laugh – something between the sound of a creaking weathercock and a corncrake, which she hurriedly smothered . . . Daniel's first feeling was hatred for a laugh which seemed to be so out of keeping with the innocent purity of her face. He suffered, too, because now that he could see her close to, he got the impression that perhaps she was not quite so young as, in his short-sightedness, he had assumed. With ardour he gazed at the freckled face which looked as though it had been scorched with flame, or as though it were formed of living sandstone. But round the mouth

and eyes, and on the skin of her throat, the signs of wear
and tear showed already visible. Young she most certainly
was, but her youth was in decline. She was touched already by the wounding arrows of a setting sun. Rather
crudely he asked her age. Staggered by the question, she
gazed at the dominating male whom she no longer saw
as a charming, flattering and gentle mannered youth.

"Do you really think I tell my age to all and sundry?"

The playful tone in which she spoke the words took
something of the sting from them. But that mattered little to Daniel. Their only effect on him was to make it
clear that she was ashamed of her age. Nothing could
alter the fact that he had not known her in her first
blooming. He followed her out on to the terrace. The
branches were dripping in a darkness filled with the
croaking of frogs.

He lit a cigarette.

"I can tell that's a Turk by the smell", she said: "give
me one."

His reply was curt.

"I hate to see young girls smoke."

Again that horrible, grating laugh rang out. Without
looking at her he proffered his tortoiseshell cigarette-case.
Noticing that she paid no attention to the gesture, he
raised his eyes. It was too dark for him to make out her
features. She was standing, and all that he could see was

that her two hands were pressing heavily on the back of a chair. Her body seemed suddenly to have sagged. The light from the drawing-room window showed only those two contracted hands. She said nothing more, but moved away from him. He could, he felt, have tracked her by the marks of blood upon the ground. He was quite sure that he had touched some raw and aching wound.

He wondered, as he lay awake that night, whether it was still raining, or whether the noise he heard was that of drops shaken by the wind from the leaves of low growing branches. He knew that he was fated to suffer, that the further he advanced in knowledge of the heart and body after which he yearned, the deeper would the mystery become – especially if she loved him. "She'll take herself to pieces, and then put herself together again, all for my benefit . . ." He could see already in his mind's eye the falsities, the knowing little touches, and he hated them in anticipation . . . Still, all he had really asked of life was that he should be drained and exhausted in an attempt to find a way, to blaze a track, through the secrets of another's intimate existence. Only to Raymond Courrège had he dared confess that all through the winter of 1916, when he lay with chattering teeth in a tent pitched on a water-logged heath, and even when, later in the same year, he went through the hell of Vauquois, his mind had been obsessed, to the exclusion of all else, by a memory – the memory of Thérèse Herlant, whom he had got to know at about that time. For him the war had been Thérèse Herlant.

Next day at luncheon he did not get so much as a glimpse of Mademoiselle de Plailly. A party of pilgrims, on their way to Lourdes, occupied a table between him and her. He heartily cursed the black, ecstatic travellers, silently accusing them of not having taken off their clothes for at least two days. He hurried through the meal, and betook himself to the bottom of the garden where he sat down on a still damp bench. The afternoon would be fine. What he had taken for a motionless cloud in the distance was no cloud, but a patch of snow.

"I'm twenty-six. Is there anything else you'd like to know?"

He gave a start, and got up. She had approached him silently like some wild animal of the woods. Her teeth glittered. Her bare arms were still marked by earlier sunburn – rather too much so. He seemed to hear beneath the piqué blouse the live pulsing of her body, as through a screen of leaves one may catch the plash of running water. Her face was radiant with youth, so radiant that he could not endure the sight of it for more than a moment. He had often stared straight and hard at the sun, and at death, but never at the face of the beloved. The eyes of love are shifting eyes. Those who gaze hard and fixedly are never lovers. She raised her beautiful arms to adjust an errant curl at the back of her head. It was as though she had suddenly extinguished a brief flare of flame. Both arms were raised, and, because of what he saw, the young man shut his eyes. She said:

"There's a way out into the open country. What about a walk? We shan't meet a soul."

That she had hinted at secrecy was later to cause him pain. There was no conceivable reason why he should not walk beside her on the road. Why, when her words were wholly innocent, should she have given him a feeling of conspiracy, why have seemed to him to be a guilty creature intent on covering her tracks, on putting some pursuer off the scent? He listened to her with only half an ear, less sensitive to her talk than to the hand which brushed his own accidentally, to the shoulder which he was growing used to seeing at such close range, to the mist of fragrance in which her body moved. She was saying that the light here was different from what it was at home. Though her home was rather less than twenty miles from Paris, it would be difficult to imagine anything more remote – an hour's drive to the station over roads rutted in autumn by wagons with their heavy load of beets . . . The lads hereabouts, in the Pyrenees, seemed to be always singing at the tops of their voices. Hadn't they kept him awake last night? At home, the young men were sodden with drink and never sang. There was no parish priest in the village, and on Sundays, because High Mass was never celebrated, the women did not dress up in their best. She didn't much care about leaving the garden, because of the men sprawling in the ditches with empty bottles beside them. Her father was fond of telling how, one winter's night, he had tripped over a carter lying in the middle of the road. The man man was dead drunk, and the rats had already begun to nibble at his face. She paused for breath, and Daniel took advantage of the silence to ask whether she spent the winters in Paris. He put the question with an absent-minded air, saying to himself the while – "I must remember the colour of her skin just at the elbow" . . . Her throat must be aching a bit! . . . all the same, she plunged into another spate of words . . . It was easy to see he didn't know Monsieur de Plailly! Widowers so often had the same sort of fads as old bachelors, didn't he think? Her father's only interest was saving money – not that, living as he did in the country and quite out of the world, there was any need for him to keep up appearances! When the war was over, he had got rid of the jobbing gardener, and did all the hoeing and weeding himself. "He looks just like a peasant . . ." It was impossible to keep a servant in the house, because whenever they had one he insisted on her looking after the pig . . . On and on she went, piling up the mountain of her grievances with an assumed air of gaiety, as though the whole thing were a joke, and at times giving rein to a grating laugh. In anybody else Daniel would have detested such vulgar chatter, such facile confidences. But in spite of her bantering tone she showed so much bitterness against her father, so much overflowing rancour, that he was appalled.

They were skirting a field when she said, – "What about a breather?"

They lay there side by side. The grass was on a level with their faces. Their hair stirred among its furrowed roots. They could hear the wind, not as a rustle of blown leaves, but as a warm, moist whisper in their ears. At intervals a lone cicada creaked its song. The clouds clung to the sides of the mountain, accentuating the deep crevices with shadow. The jade green slopes caught for a fleeting moment the sheen of sunlight, and then went dark. Seeing a stain, they asked one another was it a forest among the rolling pastures, a patch of vapour, or a black boulder? He did not look at her, but her body's heat beside him made him burn. She talked on and on, endlessly. Later it would still be too soon to remember what she had said about marriage, about young people; too soon to let the recollection rasp his nerves. Should he venture a touch? He was afraid she might resist, yet hoped she would. At last he raised himself upon his elbow and leaned his face over her, as though to drink her presence in. But suddenly she widened the distance between their bodies, and modestly drew her feet within the shelter of her skirts. He was only too familiar with this delight in being disappointed. He murmured:

Et quelle sombre soif de la limpidité

"What's that you're saying?"

"Nothing . . . just a line of poetry."

The sky clouded over. A mist came down upon the peaks. Daniel imagined to himself transfigurations on the blotted heights. They turned homewards. The young woman said nothing, and he feared her silence more than any words she might have spoken. She dragged her feet in the dust. He remembered how, on the previous evening, she had sagged before his very eyes. Was she tired? Had his attempted kiss roused her hostility? No, it wasn't that. The cloud lowering above Gisèle de Plailly was native of an unknown sky. As they passed a wayside shrine she crossed herself, and all the flowering presence of her body contracted suddenly, as though closing up. Little of religious feeling though there was in Daniel, his heart warmed to that withdrawal. He breathed in the fragrance of her devotion, could catch the scent of Spanish jasmine. Unable suddenly to bear her silence any longer, he put a casual question:

"Do you never leave your village?"

"Oh, I go to Paris sometimes."

"Alone?"

Though he shot the word at her on the same imperious tone that he had used the previous evening when he asked her age, she seemed now to be not so much annoyed as uneasy. She spoke quickly, almost breathlessly:

"No . . . yes . . . that is, I often am alone. Who should go with me? I lost my mother early. I never knew her. Would you believe it – since the war we haven't had even a horse? In order to get to the station I have to catch the local bus, at 6 a.m . . . The servant has enough on her hands with the poultry and the washing . . . I have to take the last train home at night, because it's the only one the bus meets. I find those days in Paris very long . . . there's nowhere to sit down except in the big shops . . ."

She broke off, as though realizing that she should not have said that. God in Heaven! – the idea of her wandering all day long through the jungle! It was the merest chance that he had not once picked up her scent, had not raised the hidden game! . . . As they drew near the hotel, she said it would be better if they were not seen together, because of the Pédebidous. He protested that it was the most natural thing in the world for them to have struck up an acquaintance, that there was nothing in it to give rise to gossip. But she shook her head obstinately, and begged him to go in by the garden. He resisted.

D

"The Pédebidous can jolly well think what they like!"

"And start telling tales about me when my friend comes?"

"What tales? Your friend will very soon realize that I know you."

"Will you still be here?" – she stammered.

He could see that she would have given anything to unsay those words. Faced by the look of bitter hatred in his eyes, she stood abashed, humble, gently submissive. Oh God, what agony! He felt that never again would he dare to dive straight and deep into that sleeping heart, into those treacherous waters! Had he been Raymond Courrège he would have gripped her defenceless arms, would have taken her face between his hands, would have bent her like a branch until she cracked. Without another word he left her, seeking the secret entry to the garden. Turning his head he saw her standing motionless where he had left her. Alone on the grass grown path he was swept with sudden terror as he thought of all the mud that had been stirred within him. It had spattered the young girl. Madame de Villeron . . . in imagination he could see that unknown presence clearly, down to the last detail: a stocky, swarthy creature, with yellow, liverish eyes and a hard, bold glare. He could even see how she would be dressed, could count the buttons on her mannish "tailor-made". Something Gisèle had said that

afternoon came back suddenly into his mind. At the
Abbaye-aux-Bois, when Lucille had been a senior, she
had chosen Gisèle to be her "little daughter". "You know
how it is in Convents – all the bigger girls play at being
mothers."

At dinner that night she tried quite shamelessly to
catch his eye. How imprudent she was! how little cal-
culating! He was drinking neat spirits, the better to savour
his passion. A sudden thought came to him . . . If Gisèle
were really a young girl how was it that not one word
she spoke, not one gesture she made, had hinted at marriage? She had asked no veiled questions about his family,
his "job", his income – as almost all of them did when
they spread the net. "Let me see, now, let me see", he
muttered, going back over all that they had talked about,
trying to remember what she had said about marriage.
He recalled how, at a bend in the road, when he had
asked why it was that her dear Villeron friend was not
concerned about her future, he had seen her turn pale. It
was as though he had been a doctor who feels beneath
his searching fingers that the suspected cancer has spread
more widely than he had thought. Mademoiselle de Plailly
had started on another wordy diatribe. Her father, she
had said, would make no concession. Even before the
war he could never bring himself to the point of promising to find a dowry for his daughter. He had the most

extraordinarily old-fashioned ideas on the subject of marriage, and would quote in support of his arguments, all
that had happened to the daughters of noble families way,
way, back. Not a detail did he spare her of the divorces
known to him, nor of the grubby stories lying behind
them. She had been "well posted" (that was her expression) in all the most scabrous cases of annulment which
had come before the Vatican court.

He wandered aimlessly along the dark paths, bumping
into benches, and rubbing his hands.

A cold mist had settled down on the countryside, and
Mademoiselle de Plailly was sitting in the drawing-room
with a book. When Daniel entered, she did not even raise
her eyes. He chose a chair at some distance from where
she was sitting. Suddenly her laugh rang out. She drew
his attention to the white, flattened nose of the young
man with the pimples, pressed to one of the panes of the
french window. The bloodless face vanished, and they
could hear the footsteps of the gawky creature as he paced
the verandah like a melancholy sentry.

"There are some who look like that, others . . ." There
was a bold look in the eyes she turned on him.

"Young girls quite often say", he answered her, "that
there's no need for a man to be handsome . . ."

Again, that strident laugh.

"Oh yes, it doesn't matter what he looks like so long as he's the marrying sort . . ."

The tone in which she spoke the words was unutterably vulgar.

Daniel, as though scenting danger in what she had just said, hinted that she must be far from harbouring any such thought, that only the good looking could appeal to *her*. It was then that Gisèle de Plailly gave vent to a very extraordinary remark:

"Oh", she said, "all faces bludgeon me!"

"Ugly ones, you mean?"

"Ugly ones less than others."

There was a note of brazen misery in her voice, a sort of melancholy bravado, and he found the expression of her eyes unbearable. From motives of sheer cowardice, he tried to turn her words into a joke. She must often have been in love! Her smile, the way in which she shrugged, seemed to say – a great deal oftener than you think!

With feigned gentleness he continued: "No doubt there have been some you liked more than others?"

"Don't let that bother you – I like 'em all!"

He said nothing and she went on:

"Haven't you ever felt, in a train, in a tram, in the underground, that the mere glimpse of an eye, a mouth, a hand lying in someone's lap, an ungloved hand, suddenly has the power to make one's miserable life less miserable? . . . Have you never felt that? – I have."

Behind closed eyes he visualized the underground as a human sewer sweeping her along. He made a movement towards her, his teeth clenched. She got up and went out on to the terrace. The young man with the too small heart had vanished. They felt the dark garden press like the moist nose of a nuzzling animal against their eyes, their cheeks. An electric-light bulb above their heads went on suddenly, dazzling them. At first they did not see Madame Pédebidou. She was wearing a dressing-jacket. There were two curlers in her fringe – but they heard her honeyed tones:

"Oh, I'm sorry I'm sure if I disturbed you. I only came along to see whether I could lock up."

For hours sleep would not come. He lay on his bed, trying to remember all the young girls he had ever known that he might compare them with Gisèle. Except with Marie Ransinangue, mysteriously lost, because of him, in a world of shadows which he could not penetrate, even in imagination, he had been on intimate terms with none of them. They were all plainly visible to his mind's eye: those with whom he had danced during the one winter when he had accepted invitations to balls; those whom he had met during the war, mere chance acquaintances of hospitals and billets. They all had had one trait in common – they were on their guard against him, though whether they were genuinely chaste, or were merely being careful not to "make themselves cheap", he had never been able to decide. Most of them, no doubt, had been confusing a taste for purity with the instinct of self-preservation. The mystery inherent in young girls, he thought, is born of a failure to distinguish personal interest and the stringencies of virtue. They wouldn't know, if you asked them, whether they looked on their bodies as a form of capital to be kept intact, or as a shrine within which stood some strange divinity of the yet unsullied flesh . . . "The only difference in Gisèle de Plailly that I can see, is that she has given up thinking about marriage . . . yes, that's it . . . no more, no less, chaste than the others, but less watchful, and not *hoarding* anything. All the same . . ."

He got up, crossed, bare footed, to the window, and drank in the moist and misty night like water . . .! What girl, even assuming she had a father like old Plailly, would give up all thoughts of a husband? Why, for instance, doesn't she try to get her hooks into me? She likes me. . . . Is she wholly without coquetry or cunning? Is it, perhaps, that some experience in the past has disgusted her? – or may it be that that, with the instinct common to all women, she has smelled out that I am not a marrying man? She is unlike any other young girl I have ever known. Perhaps it is because she has got no mother. She said – she had the courage to say – "all faces bludgeon me . . ."

The memory of that foolish phrase brought him a mingled sense of joy and suffering. He tried to imagine all that he might do with her, to bring his mind into line with his desires: but suddenly sleep overcame him.

A sound of incoherent muttering from the next door room awakened him. The hotel was gradually filling up. Only the evening before he had caught sight of white forms behind the netting of the tennis court. He ought to have brought his racket . . . Why shouldn't he do a bit of climbing? The real mountains were too far away. Besides, he indulged in sport only when he was not preoccupied with passion. When there was no woman to be pursued he loved to relax his body in a mood of happy vacancy. But when the fire burned hot within him, its flame was preferable to all diversion, and he could find satisfaction only in walking which, so far from turning his thoughts to other things, helped him to concentrate it on the matter in hand. In this he was different from Courrège, who would work out his emotional crises with violent exercise at the oar or in the gymnasium. For Daniel, at such times, there was no satisfaction to be found in proving himself quicker or stronger than his adversary. The spectacle of the young male animal taking pleasure in competitive struggle, produced in him a sense of boredom. Not that he hadn't met, in the bars which he frequented, young literary gents who affected an over-riding preference for boxing or for Rugby football, and celebrated those occupations in prose and verse. With some it was a sort of secret religion, a painful and ecstatic glorifying of the human body: with others, who were exhausted by debauch, an uneasy seeking for discipline and the ascetic way of life . . . Was it possible, he won-dered, to love one's body in every muscle and sinew, and thus to find a means of emptying it of passion? His own thoughts were turning now to excesses of another kind. He brooded in imagination on Marie Ransinangue, on the little country girl, wasted by fasting, thin and suffer-ing, bruising her knees upon a hard, tiled floor . . . And Gisèle? He must remember to ask her whether she played tennis. They could no doubt find a couple of rackets somewhere. A stiff game had a way of heating young bodies till they flared like torches . . . He visualized her all aflame upon the court . . . He got up, filled his tooth-glass with water, swallowed an aspirin, and waited for sleep.

Next day, Mademoiselle de Plailly was missing from her accustomed place in the dining-room. Daniel learned from the great gaunt waitress that she had gone to Lourdes for the day. He welcomed the respite. For him it repre-

sented a halting place in a descent to which he could see
no end. He was not now impatient to touch bottom. It
was enough to have caught the stench that rose from the
depths. All that now remained was for him to await the
coming of the "Villeron woman". One glance at her
would tell him more than any amount of questioning.
That ordeal once over, everything would move to its
appointed end. No longer would he hesitate to pluck the
maggoty fruit – Gisèle! He had made up his mind not to
leave the hotel until he had bitten into it and thrown it
away. A misty morning had turned to a day of great heat.
He spent it in a condition of dazed exhaustion, lying on
the thick, sappy grass between the Saint-Bavin road and
the mountain torrent. He tried to think ahead: to imagine
what it would be like, once his present tangle was straightened out, to get back to Paris, the deals and "adventures"
which Courrège would be bound to put in his way. But,
true to his rat-like character, he could not break free of
a passion so long as there was employment for his teeth!
He could never bring himself to interrupt an "affair"
once he had begun it. As, when a child he had gobbled
his books, secretly relighting the candle when he was in
bed, and never going to sleep until the last chapter had
been reached, so now he gulped each cup of passion to
the dregs. He had applied to love the Cartesian rule of
always being as resolute and determined in his actions

as he could. The first step taken, he never looked back.

On the day when he learned in conversation with the Pédebidous that Madame de Villeron was expected within the next twenty-four hours, he took a walk to the torrent. The call to Vespers was filling the oppressive Sunday air, like an ailing heart, with a broken beat. In the blazing meadows long streaks of yellow buttercups bore witness to unseen watercourses. On the grass beside the fall he could see patches of red, blue and white, the shirts of bathing boys whose cries and gurgles reached his ears from behind a screen of alders. He lay down in the narrow shadow of a hedge. Sometimes, he could catch between the branches the flash of a dripping, sun-bright body. It was as though the torpor of this sweltering day had wakened the sleeping river-sprites, as though the Great God Pan had suddenly distended his hairy chest. Like one who in a desert sucks a pebble to cheat his thirst, Daniel spoke aloud, over and over again, one single name – Gisèle, Gisèle.

He went back to the hotel along a sunken road. Suddenly, he saw her. She was coming from the direction of the fall. Her white piqué skirt was streaked with grass stains. She was carrying her hat in her hand. His first thought was that she had come from the little world of shouts, and splashings, and tumbling waters. She broke, as though in self-defence, into immediate speech.

"I've been looking for you . . . She'll be here to-morrow . . ."

He replied without looking at her:

"What's that to do with me?"

He was walking so fast that she had to run to keep up with him.

"You're staying on?" she asked.

"Certainly, if I feel so inclined."

She was out of breath: she said:

"I wish . . . I wish . . . you wouldn't take any more notice of me . . . It isn't worth your while – now . . . Please leave me alone . . ."

To that he said nothing. She had given up trying to follow him, no doubt because she did not want them to be seen entering the hotel together. He turned his head and saw her standing motionless in the full glare of the unshaded road – the same piece of wreckage that had turned and twisted in the turbulent drain of the Boulevards: a body drowned in the pushing crowds thronging the *Printemps*: a tiny wave breaking against the counters of the *Galeries Lafayette*: a traveller wandering, when the time of her train drew near, through the smoke-filled booking-hall of the Gare du Nord.

II

MADAME DE VILLERON and her daughter arrived late in the afternoon, but Daniel dared not lie in wait for them. Since the rain made walking impossible, he settled himself in the bar of the only inn. It stood in the Square. There he sat, drinking a rather too sweet white wine, and watching the heavy drops splashing on the threshold of the door, where the farmyard fowls were huddled for shelter. The wet clothing of three muleteers gave off a strong smell. A dog lay asleep under the table. A number of flies were struggling in their death-throes on strips of sticky paper. Daniel Trasis surrendered himself to the sluggish influence of the weather. Gone was all sense of urgency. The Villeron woman was there. One look at that face and he would know what lay in wait for him – and for Gisèle. He dreaded the coming revelation. Suppose she were lost to him for ever! He was so much less sure of his own strength than the companions of his squalid orgies were inclined to suspect. He knew only too well the danger of those pauses when, one passion dead, another had not come to take its place. It was what Courrège called "not being able to make the grade". He had grown used, on such occasions, to seeing Daniel in search of drugs with which to numb his pain, contemptuous of all attempts to bring, as he himself did, order into his disordered feelings, to discipline the chaotic riot of his emotions.

Daniel deliberately stayed on at the inn, and later, when he left it, kept as long as possible, to his room. He sighed with relief when, entering the restaurant at last, he saw that the women were no longer there. The three chairs at their table were pushed back. On one of them there was a pile of old *Monde Illustré* volumes on which had been perched the child whom as yet he had not seen. The three plates were stained with strawberry juice.

He spent a sleepless night. The countryside lay shrivelled under a threat of storm. Now and again the leaves rustled in a brief rising wind, and two cicadas answered one another in a stillness tense with panic. He, too, stretched out upon his bed with eyes wide open, was waiting. He could feel this final object of his insatiable hunger, Gisèle, the last of so many, dwindle and dissolve. Time and time again, face to face in solitude with some tracked, outwitted creature, conquered at last and at his mercy, he had seen the colours fade, the prey melt into nothingness. The only thing to be done when that happened, was to finish, as quickly as might be, with the dreary and inevitable routine, to go through the ritual of possession, get it all over, and then start out again on yet one more attempt to cheat his hunger with the prospect of a fresh and promising pursuit. This girl, Gisèle, whom he had never yet held in his arms, still kept him prisoner with a tender, violent obsession. Was he about to discover that she did not really exist at all? Had he merely desired her with his body only as he could have created her in the image of desire? But what he sought in her was something beyond the limits of desire, some ripple of fresh water heard long years ago, some fragrance caught in a quite different life. His passion now was impotent to model to his will the chosen creature. He feared to find her guilty of the last, worst, treachery – that of being someone other than he had thought her.

Since he had gone to bed without closing the shutters, the dawn light woke him. He could not sleep again, and the idea came to him that he might steal a march on the heat of the day by plunging into the fresh light of the early hours. The clock in the hall was striking seven. A woman was just entering the hotel. She was small, and wore a dark coloured straw hat. Her face was grey and creased, and her pale blue eyes had the look of puddles of still water, of patches of sky reflected in a rut. As he walked along the road he remembered how much he had loved the short summer nights in Paris, the twittering of waking birds in the Bois, the cool draughts of milk at the Pré-Catalan – and then rowing with Raymond on the deserted lake.

A stormy sun was already uncomfortably hot. The meadow grass was still too wet for sitting, and he looked about for somewhere to rest. Finally, he lay down in a flutter of white butterflies on a mown field. Then, he got up again, and skirted a hedge in which the wild roses had more flowers than leaves. He hated this happy country scene, and dreamed with anticipatory pleasure of the Paris that would welcome him on the evening of his return, with a twinkle of illuminated signs; of the room where he need never feel alone; of the long, silent, happy hours which he would spend there while the house was set shuddering by the nearby Underground, so that it seemed a living creature.

It was very late when he entered the restaurant. He dared not look at the table where he knew that *they* were sitting. After a while, however, he did raise his eyes. Gisèle, in her accustomed place, was cutting up meat for a pasty-faced little girl with lashless eyelids, whose thin hair was drawn back from her brow by the sort of round comb which children wore in 1890. She was perched on top of a pile of *Le Monde Illustré*, and held herself very upright. At his enemy he could not bring himself to look. She was seated opposite and had, no doubt, already taken stock of him. At long last, however, he did venture a glance, and thought at first that his eyes were deceiving him. He had built up so detailed a picture of the unknown female that he could not bring himself to believe that this retiring little woman – whose grey, creased face, and eyes like puddles of blue water he had already seen that morning – could possibly be the redoubtable amazon of his creation, with hair growing low upon her forehead, and sultry eyes beneath a pair of heavy brows – in short, the *Villeron woman*. But, unobtrusive though this stranger was, she had one definite advantage over *his* Villeron – she was alive, sitting only a few feet from him, crumbling her bread. Slowly, the image conjured up by his imagination faded, in the atmosphere engendered by the humble creature whose limpid gaze came more than once to rest upon him, not, he thought, in a wholly casual way. The two women were talking very little to one another, even though they were such close friends, and the little girl was too well-behaved a child to speak at meals. Not once did Mademoiselle de Plailly try to catch his eye in the mirror, but ate quickly, with her head bent over her plate. She too, on a sudden, had become a different person. As when a lamp, when it is brought into a room, changes the quality of light falling upon a face, and "brings out" aspects of it till then unnoticed, so did the presence of this retiring little woman with the eyes of watery blue, shed an illumination on Mademoiselle de Plailly which had the effect of turning her into a stranger. Daniel, moved only by desire, had never seen more in her than

E

a young woman with a troubled past, but this unknown
newcomer had clearly been able to work a transforma-
tion, as a result of which her young companion showed
as somebody wholly different, of whose person and nature he was ignorant. He remembered how, when he had
gone one summer to visit Raymond Courrège on his
native Norman heath, that young man had shown, in
the presence of his mother and sister, as someone far removed from the prowling beast who was his friend. He
had appeared in so new a light when seen as son and
brother as to be scarcely recognizable. In just such a way
did Madame de Villeron, merely by being there, reveal
an utterly strange Gisèle.

He knew that he lacked the power to classify people.
The reason for this no doubt was that he himself, as Courrège so often said, intending a compliment, was not a
"type", not a "mass-produced article". His life in Paris
was loosely articulated and undefined. He never cast anchor in any clearly marked piece of water, and, conse-
quently, had failed to gain that experience which might
have enabled him to "place" a woman at the first glance.
He was quite incapable now of linking this Madame de
Villeron with any species known to him. She sat at her
table, pouring out water, first for the child, then for
Gisèle, with the authority of an elder sister. After luncheon he found himself on the terrace with the two ladies,

and came out just in time to see the elder lay her needle-
work down on her lap, and ask a question of Gisèle, who
blushed fiercely and embarked upon a flood of words.
He guessed that her explanations were a form of self-
defence. Once again he was conscious in himself of the
mutterings of that jealousy which the unexpected look
of the Villeron woman had, for the space of a few hours,
side-tracked. In spite of the heat, he wandered away into
the garden under the blind eyes of the sleeping windows.
He looked at the shutters of Gisèle's room, and of her
friend's, which hid from him the mysteries of their siesta.
All the imagined horrors with which he had equipped
the Villeron woman of his creation, he now began to
attribute to the tiny woman with the limpid eyes. Pain
had once more clamped down on him. If only he, too,
could have slept! To sleep would have been better than
to live in the presence of a weary and exhausted Cybele.

A shutter on the ground floor creaked, and Madame de
Villeron's little girl appeared. She advanced with caution,
and the jerky movement of her head put him in mind of
a bird. She was shading her eyes with one hand against
the glare. With the other she clutched a doll. Hot though
it was she was wearing stockings and long sleeves. Her
high forehead, to which the round comb gave an appearance of excessive baldness, made her look older than her
age. She descended the steps very carefully, so as not to

wake her doll. At the bottom she stopped, and again raising one hand to the level of her brows, inspected the empty garden where the long grass was alive with a vibration of butterflies. The sun caught a medal which she wore on a chain round her skinny neck. Never before had Daniel paid attention to a child, but now he half closed his eyes the better to observe the little girl. For a few seconds she stood staring at her short shadow broken by the steps. Then, suddenly, Gisèle's shutters were pushed open, and Mademoiselle de Plailly leaned out. She saw Daniel, and then, the child.

"Marie!" she cried, "who told you you could get up? Come back at once, miss!"

There was an edge to her voice. A hint of uneasiness, almost of distress, sounded in her words. A combination of fear and anger gave to them that stridency which, as a rule, was noticeable only when she indulged in outbursts of loud laughter. After one last look at the garden the child turned obediently back, slipped between the shutters, and disappeared.

Daniel too, shut himself in his bedroom and tried to sleep. But soon, too restless to wait until the heat should have diminished, he ventured out into the glare of the road, and set off along the path which, a day or two before, had led him to the country church with its imprisoned lilies. He sat down at the back of the building on a bench which stood near the door. There were no lilies now in the rustic vases, but roses. As before, he felt the darkness on his forehead like a much loved hand. Slowly his eyes grew accustomed to the dimness, and he noticed, before the railing of the choir, a woman's form, prostrate and motionless. The sight of such an abandonment of faith filled him with wonder. He tried to remember whether he had ever felt anything at all like it, and recalled the mood of mockery in which, after Communion, he had gazed at Jean Péloueyre hiding his weasel face in grubby hands.

A clock was ticking quietly in the darkness of this cowbyre – a cow-byre of Epiphany made sweet with the scent of incense and of myrrh. He was happy in the knowledge that he was suffering no longer, and astonished at the prolonged presence of the woman. At last she bowed her head in deep obeisance till it touched the pavement which, no doubt, her lips saluted. Then she got up and walked towards the door. At that moment he saw that it was Madame de Villeron. He had thought of her as still sleeping behind the closed shutters of two communicating rooms. She too, recognized him. He caught the expression of astonishment in the liquid eyes she fixed on him, but let her pass.

Who was she? For a moment he felt reassured by the spectacle of so much piety. In turn he left the shadowed church. He half expected to meet the dusk of the descending evening, but when he emerged the crumbling walls of the poor village were still hot with sunlight. But the hour was close at hand which would bring relief to earth and human flesh alike. The same cracked dissonance sounded in the clang of sheep-bells and of Angelus . . . He remembered how on one occasion, when they were together on the terrace, Gisèle, when the lightning flashed had said : "If Lucile were here, she would want to light a candle." "Heavens!" he had muttered, "so she's bigoted and superstitious, too, is she?" – and at that his peace of mind had taken flight.

At dinner that evening, though his eyes did not once encounter those of his enemy, he was alert for her every gesture. She was wearing a nondescript sort of bodice innocent of all adornment, with a high tulle collar. He noticed when she walked to the door that her watch was tucked into her black silk girdle in an outmoded fashion. Perhaps she was younger than he had at first supposed. It was probably the only time in all his life that he had paid any attention to a woman not shaped for love – a woman of the kind that Raymond Courrège was fond of describing as being "non-edible". Not that she was ill looking. Those eyes of hers, pools of water, patches of sky, were even attractive. Her worn and battered face must, at eighteen, have glowed with youth. But even in

those days her body must, surely have been of the kind
which even the most degraded could not strip in imagination. *Touch me not!* was, in her case, inadequate: *Let no
base thought come near me!* – that was the type she was. To
himself Daniel murmured: "but what sweetness of authority!"

Strange fancies, indeed! – he must be mad! "The dregs
of womanhood, that's nearer the mark: the dregs of
womanhood!" Smoking in the garden he soundlessly
applied to her epithets of unspeakable vileness.

There was a patter of running feet, a sound of laboured
breathing. Gisèle came hurrying towards him, her head
turned to see whether she was being followed. He had
eyes only for the lines of her body, for the heavy mass of
her hair. But he could hear her panting, and could feel
that she was crying – as from the fragrance of a garden
in the dark one can guess the falling drizzle. She said:

"I've been looking for you . . . I saw the glow of your
cigarette . . . I wanted to say . . . but you won't listen to
me . . . I wanted to ask you . . . you told me once there
was nothing to keep you here, that you could easily settle
down somewhere else . . . I wanted to ask you to go . . .
to go right away . . ."

She was crying bitterly. He would dearly have loved
to follow blindly the instinct which always told him what
to do when he was faced by a woman in tears: to yield

to a desire to comfort her, to lull her into sleep, to taste on her cheeks the sea-salty flavour of her grief. But he said nothing and she continued:

"What must you be thinking? – so many things, and all so far from the truth . . . How can you possibly understand that I am asking this of you because, because – you have become for me . . ."

She left the weighty phrase unfinished. No young man ever tires – no matter how often it may be repeated – of the sharp pleasure of a woman's surrender, can never have enough of bowed head and willing lips. For the prowling male defences can never be too often breached. But on this occasion Daniel Trasis thought that he discerned something kept back, something left unsaid, in the avowal which made his prey seem infinitely precious. That quality in her which, from the very first, he had found so appealing, that freshness for which he so fiercely thirsted, came to his senses now like the scent of mint in summer dusks, like the smell of foaming water as it comes over a fall. He drew her to him, breathing in the fragrance of warm tears like raindrops striking the parched earth. He could feel against his body the very being of the hot, moist darkness. To himself he said: "In a moment now I shall know why she asked me to go away . . ." But even as his lips moved gently down her bitter tasting cheeks towards her mouth, uneasiness awoke within his mind: "Why is she so insistent on my going?" On the very confines of her parted lips he caught his breath, broke from her, turned away his face, and lit a cigarette.

"Gisèle!"

An anxious voice was calling from beneath the trees.

"Gisèle!"

She moved away from him, tidied her hair, and with an excessive assumption of calmness, of indifference, replied:

"Here I am, Lucile."

"Where?"

"At the bend in the path – I was just taking a breath of fresh air" (then, in a low voice, to Daniel) – "throw away your cigarette – don't move!"

He stood there motionless, while she hurried in the direction of Madame de Villeron, saying as she went:

"Did you think I was lost? – you always think I'm lost . . . No, I'm not a bit cold, really I'm not."

He realized that Madame de Villeron had thrown a coat round the girl's shoulders. He stayed where he was, alone conscious of his solitude, and looking back over his own brief life, remembering a room in an isolated farm, the exact point on the floor, close to the mantelpiece where his father had collapsed, the stink of alcohol and cigar-smoke downstairs, the dirty pane to which Uncle Louprat used to press his congested face, the dormitory window through which Jean Péloueyre had gazed up at the stars, the sandy grass on the edge of a great meadow circled by gloomy pines, caravans moving across the desert of the sky, a car upon a road under enemy fire, blood dripping on his hand from the stretcher slung above his head, Paris with its jazz, and two bodies clamped together in a motionless shuffle, the leather upholstered bars where he had so often sprawled, all in, with his head on the shoulder of some woman at whose face he had never so much as looked – the mad rush through the dawn emptiness of Paris in the Hispano, with five other fellows, and a woman who had passed out or who was sleeping – and he saw, too, with his mind's eye a little country-girl on her knees, scrubbing the red tiles of a Carmelite Convent, with, close beside her, an earthenware bowl of water, and on the whitewashed wall, a crucifix.

Two days of blazing heat passed without his so much as catching a glimpse of the ladies. He wandered about the countryside, lunching at chance inns, and never entering the hotel dining-room at night, until the others had finished their meal. He was suffering both in body and in spirit. It was not the city, with its light signs and its pavements, its promenades and dance music, that woke in him the prickings of desire. The body soon grows deaf to all those raucous appeals of pleasure. But, in the country, in the season of sunlight and storms, the flesh is subject to the universal law. To fight against it in oneself is to claim the power to hold back the tides, to stop the flowing waters, to hold in check the movement of the rivers – of those that chatter gaily down the hills, of those that, all unseen, swell the growing plants with sap. One might just as well try to move mountains. Who was it claimed we can move mountains? What lunatic was it who had demanded of men that they should move mountains? Like a mad dog, Daniel haunted the banks of the stream, and sometimes, like a man whose clothing has caught fire, flung himself, a living torch, upon its surface.

On the third day, he returned to the hotel about five o'clock. Little Marie, in her orphanage smock, with her hair pressed back from her forehead by the round comb, was running after a white butterfly on the lawn, slapping down her straw hat on the flower from which the butterfly had just departed. The pimply young man, whose heart was too small for his body, was following her movements with an attentive eye. He was so bony that the legs of his trousers looked as though there was nothing inside them. Marie, seeing that the two were looking at her, moved away. The pallid youth followed her. The expression of his face was that of a hesitant half-wit.

"I bet you won't catch me!" – he said, and began to run about the grass, making circles round her, and per-

forming so strange, so macabre, a dance that the solemn child could not keep from laughing. The laugh was a grating screech – a horrible sound which Daniel had heard before. He turned away his head, looking for Gisèle, hearing her laugh but nowhere seeing her. Meanwhile, the young man with the small heart was jumping up and down, trampling the sappy grass, and reducing the cicadas to silence. He was panting, and his legs, which seemed made of wire, expanded and contracted in a series of funereal capers. On and on grated that too familiar laugh. The pimply dancer pretended to be a jumping jack. Gasping for breath he called out to the child – "They called me piece of string when I was at school!"

Suddenly overcoming her shyness, she said:

"You're Mister String – how d'you do, Mister String!"

She was as though possessed, helpless in the grip of a fit of laughter. Daniel Trasis, leaning against a chestnut tree, was hurriedly contriving reasons for the sound: "She's caught it from Gisèle. They must see more of one another than I had supposed . . . children are just like monkeys, for ever imitating . . ." This he kept on saying to himself, but all the while a terrible realization was dawning in his mind. He saw now that for a long time past Gisèle's secret had been no secret at all, that the laughter of this freckled child had nothing to teach him that he did not know already – the meaning of that laughter which was still grating through these moments of the afternoon's end, like the sound of the last cicada.

The dancer, stretched flat, face downwards on the grass, had ceased to move – a broken doll. The child, thoughtful for one brief moment, looked at him, then turned away, as though she had accomplished what had been given her to do, just now, just here.

No longer conscious of his suffering, Daniel reached his room just ahead of the first clap of thunder. He pushed the shutters open, flung himself upon the bed, and closed his eyes, saying to himself – "you've no proof, not a scrap of evidence". But what need had he of proof, possessing this certainty? The better to feel the smarting wound, he said, over and over again: "an unmarried mother, an unmarried mother!" – then he got up, gazed at his reflection in the mirror, and spoke in a low voice: "Why should I care? What if she has made a fool of me? It's not too late, I'll have her just the same." This'd teach him to feel respect for women! If Raymond had been here now, he'd soon have restored things to their proper perspective. "The only thing that matters", he'd have said, "is to find out whether the kid has spoiled her body." To some women motherhood gives a new bloom, though those who can withstand the damaging results of pregnancy are few. In a mocking voice he declaimed a line – "To me you will give your outraged breasts" – then burst into laughter which ended on a sob. Profligate though he was he wept for lost innocence. He felt no jealousy. The knowledge that another had possessed Gisèle caused him no suffering. His only thought was that all the ways of passion were now known to her. He closed the shutters again, so as not to have to see the blown and blustery grasses, the beaten alders loud with the surge and battery of falling waters – then shut the window that he might not catch the scent of mint wafted towards him from the river bank which he had once seen dotted with the blue and red shirts of bathing boys – that bank of trodden greenery where, on an afternoon, he had watched a girl hurrying towards him, damp with sweat, while, behind a screen of branches, young bodies all a-glitter with the sun and water, ran at play.

Useless that refrain – "I'll have her yet!" Desire had lost its power. Had Gisèle been with him now what would he have asked of her? Would he have beaten her, or would he have leaned his head upon her shoulder, and cried? More than all else, he felt the need to see her. He went straight to her door and, without knocking, flung it open. The room was empty, but, in spite of the open windows, the smell of the red-haired woman who was no longer there, rose up to greet him. He walked across to the narrow, virgin bed. A "wrapper" lay festooned across a chair. Two slippers were standing on the floor.

A long frame of red leather displayed the portrait of an old man with the look of a vulture – Monsieur de Plailly, obviously – several pictures of Marie at various ages, and one of a serious-looking young woman who must be Lucile de Villeron fresh from her convent school. His mood grew calm and tender. What came now to his lips was not the hateful phrase "unmarried mother", but something quite different, something mystical, mysterious, and uttered with no thought of blasphemy – "virgin mother". Despite her fall, the girl whom he had loved was still a living presence in his heart. Why? He remembered how he had been accustomed to scan the faces of young prostitutes, trying to find some trace of lost virginity. His mind went back to the Russian girl with short cropped hair, whom he had met in a shady dance-hall frequented by effeminate young men. She had refused the advances made to her by Raymond Courrège, but had willingly gone home with Daniel. A summer dawn had been brightening the room by the time his casual love had fallen asleep. He had stayed a long time watching on the confines of her slumber, gazing at the face on which the purity of childhood had left, in passing, a mysterious radiance. In just such a way was he now conscious of a flood of memories as he stood beside the narrow bed of innocence. The noiseless coming on of dusk was musical with birdsong, with the sound of stable clocks, and the ringing of the Angelus. Gisèle! The scent that floated in from the garden was less strong than the fragrance left by her nightly sleep within these walls. He turned down the counterpane and, kneeling by the bed, buried his face in the pillow, repeating to himself a refrain remembered from his nights of roaming: "I want to sleep: I'd rather sleep than live." Quite motionless, fearing that anguish would return if he so much as stirred a finger, he breathed in the freshness of her sheets.

"What are you doing here?"

He got to his feet and saw Madame de Villeron, pale-faced and rigid, watching him. It was as though the humble, self-effacing woman had grown in stature. She looked like a hen swelling and bristling up her feathers in defence of her young.

"Leave this room at once: if you don't, I shall call out."

The Villeron of Daniel's earlier imagination had suddenly come to life in the flesh. At sight of her thus transformed, he felt a bitter pleasure. He was wholly master of himself, quite sure that he was the stronger of the two. He stood there studying her.

"I can only think", she stammered, "that you have mistaken the room."

His reply to that was insolent:

"I certainly did not think, Madame, that it was yours."

"Go away, or I shall summon help: go away at once, go!"

He answered tartly that she was not in her own room.

"But I am in my friend's – in Mademoiselle de Plailly's." He smiled, and looked his adversary straight in the skyblue eyes. He saw in them the sudden oncoming of pain, and quietly said:

"Mademoiselle de Plailly is my friend too."

Whatever he may have hoped for from this thrust, the sight of her contracted features and fluttering eyelids surprised him. When she brought out, at last, that mere casual acquaintanceship gave him no right to be there, he struck the fatal blow.

"Who told you that there is no more between Mademoiselle de Plailly and myself than mere casual acquaintanceship?"

He felt that the wound he had given her was mortal. Her face was putty-coloured; the twin pools of blue were misted over. The realization that he had drawn blood, so far from calming him, urged him to strike again.

"I know now what you are . . ."

Daniel Trasis was no man of the world. He had never undergone that training which, in a man of the world, destroys the natural connexion between thought and speech, between act and feeling. He said again:

"I know now . . . you are . . ."

F

He dared not finish the sentence. Had Raymond Cour-rège been there at that moment, he would have recognized his friend. His cast-off mistress would have recognized him, and all the many women whom he had dragged through the mud. Feeling the brooding stare of this brute fixed upon her, Madame de Villeron recoiled towards the window.

"I don't know what you mean . . ." she said in an uncertain voice.

"You're pretending not to understand. Perhaps I should do you the justice of believing that you *think* you have behaved well to this poor child, but I know that you have taken advantage of her wretchedness, that . . ."

Again he stopped short. It was as though he were weighing a stone in his hand before throwing it. Fear must have killed the anger in her, for she spoke now as to a madman who must be quieted:

"Control yourself, sir, or, perhaps, I should say, let us both control ourselves . . . We will speak of these matters some other time when we are less worked up. I admit that I may have been somewhat too violent . . ."

Thinking that she was mocking him, he asked in a flat voice whether it mattered so little to her to know what others thought. He had moved close, and was penning her against the window. Words bubbled up within him. How he would have liked to fling them at her, one by one! But some unknown hand had him by the throat, strangling the filthy epithets upon his lips, preventing him, against his will, from uttering them. Meanwhile, faced by the pressure of his fury, she made no movement, but stood her ground like a martyr protected by legions of angels. She stilled the beating of her heart, and, with a lucid eye, stared at her shamefaced tormentor. No matter what it might cost, she must find out precisely how far this lean wolf had gone in his designs. He could no longer endure the fixity of her eyes which once again had become calm and courageous, had become pools of rainwater, patches of serenest blue. A touch of anger still there may have been in them, but, more than anger, astonishment, and perhaps, a terrified concern. In a flash of memory he had recalled the look he had seen in nurses' eyes . . . Still trembling, leaning for support against the window frame, but resolute, she spoke:

"I have no idea what charge you are bringing against me . . ." Pull yourself together, I beg. Would you like me to see you back to your own room?"

There was calmness in her voice, there was compassion. This woman was certainly not trying to put him off the scent. Sobered now, stunned, bewildered by the evidence before him, and incapable of entertaining the least doubt of what he saw, he said within himself: "She hasn't understood . . . she doesn't understand."

No, she had not understood. For hours he might have pelted her with stones, and still she would have said – "I don't know what you mean". The chestnuts at her back, in the evening sun, were full of birdsong. Suddenly he was seized with horror at the thought of what he had so nearly said to this woman who was ignorant of evil. Whence she had come so utterly untouched by the knowledge of sin, he could not say, but what she was *not* he now saw clearly, and, in a flash, knew from what an infinite distance he was looking at her. Wordless, ashamed, he stood there, choking back his tears. It was then that in the simple words of simple folk, she spoke kindly to him:

"Have a good cry: it'll do you good . . . let yourself go, and when you've had your cry out, we will talk."

She fixed him with her unclouded gaze, and he, obedient, as he ever was, to an inner command that he should conform to his enemy's idea of him, began to feel that his heart had grown lighter, and been purged of vileness, had regained its pristine purity. He had turned slightly away. One hand was pressed against his eyes, and he did not see Madame de Villeron go back to her own room. He heard a spoon tinkle against glass, and then her voice speaking with authority:

"Drink this – just a drop of Valerian: it doesn't taste as bad as it smells."

He had a horror of medicines, but could no more refuse her now than he could have refused in a hospital during the war.

"And now, sir, let us leave this room. She may be back at any moment. We will have our little talk in the garden. After this absurd scene we each owe the other an explanation."

He followed her obediently – aware of the note of motherly solicitude in her voice, and freed from the fear that she might have grasped his meaning. He felt almost happy, and too much overwhelmed as yet to guess how determined she would be to keep from him her secret knowledge of Gisèle. Of what a kind that knowledge was he had not the least idea. There are bonds other than those of the flesh by which two persons may be strongly linked. Between Madame de Villeron and Gisèle there existed ties less tender, but not less powerful, than those which Daniel had supposed. If, as he had meant to do, he had flung disgusting insults in her teeth, and if she had caught their meaning, her attitude would not have been in any way changed. She would have stood her ground, and not one inch would she have yielded. He was a stranger to any such feeling as passion for another's safety, when danger threatens, or of the obstinate fight in which a champion can engage when the question at issue is to keep the menaced prey from yielding. All the same,

he followed in the footsteps of this strange woman, cling-
ing to her, and thrilled with a delicious hope. He had
been wrong about her: might he not also have been
wrong about Gisèle? After all, what proof had he against
her other than the timbre of a laugh? Maybe he had only
to look at people to make them vile. But Gisèle was
innocent, and he was going to be assured of that innocence.

So wholly absorbed was he by the prospect, that he
quite failed to realize that Madame de Villeron was, in
her turn, studying him. She was struck with amazement
that he should suddenly have grown so calm: she was
intent only on discovering what place this coarse male
creature occupied in the life of that wandering sheep
whom she had lost and found again, just as she was about
to lose her way once more.

They had reached a distant pathway in the garden
over which the evening shadows were already gathering.

"It was I, sir, who first lost my temper. I provoked you
to strike back. But I should like you to understand something of what I was feeling. Her parents entrusted her to
me. You don't, I think, realize that I am her spiritual
guardian, nor even know the meaning of the phrase. Are
you of those who believe in life everlasting? I think you
maybe, since you are capable of spending a whole hour
alone in a country church ... Oh yes, I saw you there the

other day. When you told me that there was more between my friend and you than mere casual acquaintanceship, I was nearly out of my mind. But though we are
strangers, I trust you, and I know that you will not de-
ceive me."

She spoke in accents of persuasion, and as one having
authority. It was quite obvious that she was a born director of consciences, and cleverer than any priest would
have been in the handling of souls. She was one of those
women for whom hospitals and welfare centres are so
many storage tanks and reservoirs of human beings
waiting to be saved. As but a while back, so now, the
desire to overcome, and to convince, seemed to give her
a greater stature. How much her stature seemed to have
increased! He stammered out that what he had said had
been prompted by crude bravado: that he had never ad-
dressed a word to the young girl that had not been
dictated by feelings of respect: that though, without intention, he might have let her see that he felt drawn to
her, he had never said so.

The woman was watching him intently. He could not
endure the almost excessive clarity of her gaze. At last
she said:

"I believe you."

She stood there motionless, her right hand supporting
her left elbow, one finger to her cheek, her head leaning

slightly to one side, and seemingly deep in thought. In her black girdle there was a silver watch-chain from which depended a cluster of medals and a golden cross. The high tulle collar, which reached to her ears and projected even into her scraped-back hair, gave her a stiff and awkward look. Daniel was busy with his thoughts: "She's going to ask me about my financial position, about my family: she is probably considering my suitability as a possible husband for Gisèle . . ." and already he was wondering what reply he ought to make. But Madame de Villeron, as though talking to herself, said:

"I've got rid of my fear . . . all the same, it was wrong of me to leave the child alone in an hotel. Others might have been less considerate than you were . . ."

He answered with a touch of sharpness that Mademoiselle de Plailly was old enough to look after herself.

"No doubt . . . but, you see, she knows so little of the world. She is not like other girls. Her family lives in a remote countryside, out of touch with everybody, and almost without a penny."

Very quietly she recapitulated all that Gisèle had complained of in her father. But there was no hint of violence in her voice. She spoke like one who wishes to say nothing that might harm a fellow mortal. Daniel realized that her every word had been carefully chosen with the object of discouraging him from pursuing any idea he might have entertained of marrying Gisèle. But clearly it was not jealousy that prompted her. She said what she said in the role of an unhappy guardian intent on keeping a prowling male at bay. There was nothing to warn her that the young man listening to her words had guessed the secret, nor that, with every word she spoke, she was confirming, unknown to herself, the hideous knowledge that he had acquired. She described the girl's home life, its concealed austerities, her father's constant obsession with impending destitution. He must, thought Daniel, be one of those million imbeciles who, for the last forty years, had been increasingly impoverished by the State and the big banks, who had been caught in the toils of Russian loans and Italian railways. Now, the poor fleeced sheep, bogged down in his half acre of land, was slowly dying of want, passing the time in weeding his flower beds, while his daughter spent whole days wandering aimlessly in Paris. He bit back the words which rose to his lips – "I know all that – don't go on!" Perhaps, even though in the darkness beneath the trees she could not see his ravaged face, she guessed at the despair which could find no words, for suddenly she stopped speaking.

"Why" – he muttered – "are you so keen that I should give her up?"

"I am not keen, as you put it; I have no right to be."

"Oh yes, you are! – you want me to give her up. Tell me your reasons – if you dare!"

A cry broke from her:

"Would to God my poor Gisèle might find a man who could save her!"

He hung his head. A bell rang out, summoning them to the evening meal. Madame de Villeron stood looking at him, amazed that he had not asked the question she had been expecting: "Is she, then, so far lost that she needs saving?" But, with his eyes cast down, he asked no question. When the bell sounded for the second time, they began to hurry. A shrill little voice was calling to them.

"Mémé!"

Madame de Villeron called back:

"Coming!"

"Mémé! Mémé! Dinner's ready!"

The little girl, all out of breath, appeared at a turn in the path, saw Daniel, and stopped. Her freckled face was slightly flushed with running. One red lock of hair was sticking to her over-prominent forehead, which was damp with sweat. One of her stockings had fallen down, and revealed a skinny knee, marked with a scratch.

Shyly she said again: "Dinner's ready, Mémé."

With an irritable movement of the head, and as though speaking to himself, he said in a low voice:

" Surely she's old enough to have learned to say Mamma?"

He tried in vain to catch his enemy's eye. But it would not meet his own, and he broke into a long and mocking laugh. Without a word, Madame de Villeron snatched up the child. Holding her tight in her arms she started towards the house, almost at a run. But soon she had to slow down. Breathless, bent, weighed down by her living load, she slowly, painfully, pursued her way.

Daniel remained where he was, shivering in the damp darkness. Tonight he would go without his dinner. He would wait until he could be sure of slipping into his room without meeting anybody. Thinking of nothing, listening to the beating of his heart and the gentle rustling of leaves, he was conscious of a sensation which he had often felt in earlier days when playing at hide and seek, when Marie Ransinangue was "He" and passed him by as he hid from her, holding his breath. He had known, in those days, how to remain completely silent, how to freeze into utter immobility till he was no more than a scrap of living matter which only the wind could move: nature, the only opium.

As soon as it was quite dark, he made his way back to the hotel. As he passed under the Pédebidous' window, he caught the sound of Madame de Villeron's voice. She was settling her own and Gisèle's bills, and ordering the 'bus for the next morning. They were leaving! "You've got one night left! One whole night – a lifetime!" That was what Raymond Courrège would have said . . . But no, thought Daniel, he would not dispute over this piece of human wreckage with the woman who was so intent on saving her. He was not, he told himself, giving up much. After all, the Gisèle of his desires had no real existence. What he had adored in her had never been anything more than a mirage of lost purity. Not that he wouldn't have liked to cheat his hunger with the body he had thought to be untouched, untarnished . . . But he would fight down that hunger. If it was now his pleasure to put no obstacle in the way of the sentimental and idiotic Villeron woman, surely he was free to do so? There was no reason why he should be condemned for ever to behave like an animal in rut. Once back in Paris he would have plenty of time in which to stifle his memories. In imagination he saw himself rushing to the city which, in this month of August, would be an empty maze of hot asphalt and paving stones, a place where all passion could quickly find its satisfaction. The moon was rising. He felt hungry, went to the inn, where he interrupted a rustic chorus, and ordered some pâté, and a bottle of the white wine of which he was so fond. He ate and drank: he ate in order to drink – in solitude, because the muleteers and their women had drifted into the billiard-room next door. When he left, the moon had washed the sky clean of stars, clothing the mountain sides in velvety shadows, causing the cocks to crow and the dogs to bark their worship of its face.

He fell into that light sleep which comes with moonlit nights, when the droning of a fly, the rustling of leaves, the dogs at their ritual exercise of baying at the moon, the endless quiver of a waking world, form links which bind to universal life the bodies of young creatures who lie at length, burning more brightly hot in the darkness than all the incandescent worlds. A quiver, a puff of air, wakened him, as though the lime had stretched its branches through the open window to wave about his bed. A flood of milky light was rippling across the floor and on to his bed. It threw a white radiance on the doorway. He heard a breath which was not the breath of the countryside, a rustling that was not the sound of leaves in the darkness. Then he saw, beneath his door, the corner of a piece of paper which an invisible hand was trying to push into the room. Someone must be there, out in the dark and narrow entry which separated his room from the main corridor. The paper shone in the moonlight like a speck of snow. With one bound he was out of bed. He ran to the door and flung it open. Someone, squatting on the further side, straightened up, a shadowy shape breathing audibly, a shape of flesh and blood. Because of the dishevelled hair, at first he did not recognize her. The small, diminished face confused him. At first he did not see it was Gisèle, and when, at last, he realized who was there, it was by the sound of her voice, rather than by her features, that he knew her.

Her words, when at last they came, were breathless, halting.

"It was just . . . that I wanted . . . to leave a letter . . . for you. . . *She* insisted that I should go without saying good-bye . . . without a word. She told me that you knew . . . that you couldn't help knowing. . . For all I know, she may have betrayed me . . ."

She broke off in a sudden fit of crying. Her face was hidden in her hands, and the tears were trickling between her fingers. The loose sleeves of her dressing-gown had slipped back when she raised her arms, and they were bare. But his mind at that moment was busy with a fantastic thought: 'How lucky that I'd got my pyjamas on!' . . . He pulled the flimsy material across his naked chest. Then, in a low voice, he said:

"You mustn't stay here a moment longer!"

There was just time, but only just, for her to get away from him.

"I know . . . but swear to me you'll read this letter . . . I don't want you to have horrible thoughts about me . . .

I couldn't bear that. Read what I've written. You'll see
from that how miserably unhappy . . ."

"Go away!"

"I will. I only wanted to leave this letter for you. I'm
not sorry you caught me, because it gives me a chance of
saying good-bye, in spite of Lucile. Would you believe
it, she's making me take the early 'bus so as to catch the
first train, so as to be quite sure I shan't see you again . . .
But I have seen you, Daniel."

Having uttered these last words in a tone of mingled
resentment and triumph, she came a few steps into the
room, and moved towards him.

"Go away!" he said again in a low voice. But she did
not stop. He retreated to the window in such a way as to
keep the bed between them. The moon was sinking. The
meadows on this summer night were making a contin-
uous murmur like the sea. Washed by the living waters
of the stream they gave off a smell as strong as that of
ocean wrack and seaweed. He heard her murmured
words:

"The child . . . yes . . . I have explained it all in my
letter, you must read it there . . ."

"I *will* read it – but for Heaven's sake, don't stay in this
room!"

He had not yet fallen upon the willing prey, because
for the time being – but how long would it last? – his

chief desire was not to upset the good and honourable schemings of the woman whose name he used now as though it were a talisman:

"Go back to Lucile de Villeron, before she finds out what has happened . . . in the long run I should be only your undoing . . . she alone can give you safety . . ."

At these words, the girl blazed into fury: so she'd got round *him* now, had she! . . . He called her Lucile, did he! Of course she had a will of iron, no one would deny that, but this everlasting mania for protection was enough to drive one mad. It was only in order to levy a sort of filthy blackmail that Lucile had taken pity on *her*!

"She uses penitence as a weapon against me."

Daniel could hear inside himself the first growlings of the famished, unclean animal. He took a step forward. The delicious, the desperate moment had come when two beings, though they may still for a while put up a show of resistance, know that they are lost. Not yet have their bodies been flung, inextricably entwined, into the pit, but they have leaned so far over the fatal gulf that no power, of Heaven or of earth – can hold them back.

We may for days have longed to clasp another human body. The point has come when we can persuade ourselves that we have possession within our grasp. We hug and hold the prey within our arms. We burn in the furnace of our blood. Sensual magic has wrought a transference, so that we see with our hands, touch with our eyes. All resistance has ceased: at last, surrender is complete. We enter the very being of the prize. We draw in the very breath of its life, but even then we do not possess it. Our furious tide beats against another's being, dashes against a living wall, bursts through, ebbs back, but never finds the ultimate satisfaction. To ourselves we say: "I shall remember for ever this mysterious flexion of her knees, the secret loveliness of the way in which shoulder merges into breast." In vain! The ingenuities of lust are powerless. By the ways of the flesh we try to achieve the mastery of another's being. But we never do.

The song of blackbirds was heralding the dawn. So heavy was her sleep that she seemed dead. He lay there thinking of the unknown man who had first awakened her, had trained the sleeping senses to accept his will. His spirit was in torment, his body shivering with cold, being naked. Never had he felt the traffic of the flesh to be without significance (even though he had pretended to accept Courrège's doctrine that "one act is much like another act"). Always, at such moments, he had had to stifle in himself a struggling protest that rose from somewhere deep within him. But it was only now, and for the first time, that in the icy wind of early dawn, and feeling frozen to the marrow, he faced the bitter and the

G

ultimate truth that bodily love is a struggle in which there is no winner.

As the wet leaves filled with birdsong he wakened Gisèle.

"Get up, quick!"

She opened her eyes and smiled. But as she met his gaze her smile faded. She was frightened. The sated male is strong, and it is the weakness of women like Gisèle to be for ever hungry. "Once more", they think to themselves, even when they have been caressed a thousand times: "just once more so I may feel convinced that I am still desired."

He urged her to return to her room. Madame de Villeron would be up early to finish her packing. She might even go to early Mass.

Gisèle asked a question: "How am I going to find you in Paris, darling?"

So many women had asked him that, and to none of them had he given his address.

"I want to know where you live."

He hesitated, thinking of his Paris room, of how Gisèle's sweet body would make it gleam more brightly than the lamp that stood upon the floor. But could he so far defy Madame de Villeron? He felt, perhaps, that the girl's lost purity might bloom anew under the warming breath of the older woman. Then, and only then, worked on by the powers of a mysterious renewal, would Gisèle cease to be like all the others – an object that had served its turn. Even now, after this night that they had spent together, her strange limpidity remained unclouded. It was as though Gisèle de Plailly were endowed, in spite of herself, with the gift of an immortal maidenhood . . .

For the moment, however, that sense in him was vague, obscure. Besides, as always when the act had been accomplished, he was feeling ready to renounce the flesh.

"I won't go until you have given me your address! . . . And you will read that letter, won't you? I came last night only to slip it under your door . . . I should hate you to think . . . I wanted you to read it when you woke . . . Tell me you believe that."

Daniel, intently listening, whispered: "I think I can hear somebody moving in the corridor . . ."

"You must be mad, my love. You can't get your mind off Lucile. Why, it's not five o'clock."

"Gisèle, I heard somebody breathing just outside the door. Don't talk: listen."

They held their breath. The mist was noisy with the twittering of birds. They could hear nothing but the movement of the pigeons on the tiles, the peeping of a nestful of young swallows. Out on the road there was a lowing of cows.

"She's spying on us, I tell you."

Gisèle shivered under her wrap.

"At least promise that you'll write – Louvres, Seine-et-Oise. I've put it at the top of my letter. I shan't begin to live again until I've heard from you."

He promised. He pushed her towards the threshold. He followed her out into the dark entry, and opened the outer door which he kept shut so that the noises of the hotel should not reach him.

He stood there motionless, with one hand on his breast. Suddenly, at sound of a stifled cry, he ventured to set the door ajar and peep out. Then it was that he thought he saw, at the other end of the corridor, where a night lamp was still burning, the figure of Lucile de Villeron. She had just flung a long coat round the evidence of Gisèle's guilt, and was leading her away.

III

THERE can be few things worse than a second-class carriage on the Midi section of the French Railways in the height of summer. Even though the one in which Lucile and Gisèle sat facing one another was full, fresh passengers got in at every station and stood blocking the corridor. Marie was perched beside Lucile. There was coal-dust on her sweating face. She had a solemn look, and was deep in her private thoughts. Most children born outside wedlock are from their earliest years bandied about by life. Marie was no exception to this rule, and had long ago learned how to suffer in silence. Two men – dealers or travelling salesmen – had taken off their coats and loosened their collars. They had the prominent stomachs of the confirmed *aperitif* drinker, mottled faces and watery eyes. They sat with their legs well apart to facilitate the act of spitting, and regularly got out at every stop – "how about a quick one?" – exchanging civilities, putting up cheerfully with mild rebuffs – "No, this is on me, ma'am." Fortunately, they never stopped smoking, and the smell of Maryland tobacco covered others far worse which, thought Lucile, Gisèle could never have endured. But the girl was fast asleep. They had not exchanged a word since the train started. But at least the shepherd could brood over the wretched sheep now unconscious and defenceless. Her mouth was sagging like a corpse's, and round her eyes were dark circles that told of sinful and delicious weariness. Once already, Lucile had dragged her from the River of Fire. For two years she had protected her from the molten lava, and now she had fallen in again! How strenuously, thought the elder woman, she had fought to keep her safe since that now distant day when Gisèle, as a very young girl, had first awakened in her a feeling of uneasiness. On the opening day of term in the playground of the Sacré-Coeur, under its shady elms with their tar-smeared gashes, Mother de Coffen had come towards her in the pale sunshine holding by the hand a red-haired little girl. "This is your daughter, Lucile", she had said, and it was not long before Lucile had come to dominate the hot-blooded young creature. But Gisèle in her innocence had not realized that she was different from the other pupils. So ardent were her kisses that those on whom she lavished them had had to tear themselves away from her embraces. It was as though her body carried a secret of which she knew nothing, and whenever the gentlest among her mistresses and fellow-pupils repulsed her, she would burst into tears. Lucile remembered one period of summer holidays at the Plailly home (she had always spent the last two weeks of

August there with her "daughter"). Gisèle had just turned fifteen. She was a quiet little thing, with sleepy eyes and two modest plaits of hair, and spent her time playing at hide and seek, looking after her doll, and seemed entirely unconscious of her own developing body. She was pious, too, and often when she took her handkerchief from her pocket, a rosary fell out upon the ground. But in the mornings she would scarcely ever leave the terrace which overlooked the road. The butcher's boy was her friend, the carpenter's apprentice, and other youths as well. It was all very harmless – a mere mutual exchange of grins and, now and again, a bunch of flowers tossed over the wall. It never occurred to the young innocent that she was doing wrong. She made no attempt to hide what was going on from Lucile, until a day came when her "mother" had found it necessary to scold her because of a letter written by the lawyer's clerk which made Gisèle laugh. She remembered, too, those games of hide and seek at which nobody could ever find Gisèle. She used to look for her with a feeling of uneasiness which she never confided to anybody else. At long last the girl would appear from behind a truss of hay in the loft, with a sly look in her eyes, straw in her hair, and scarcely ever alone. The chemist's one son, and the doctor's two, would fight like cockerels, to have her on their "side". Oh, how Lucile had suffered then; what extremities of self-denial she had imposed upon herself! Bitter were the tears she shed as she prayed for the salvation of one who was still so ignorant of vice that she dared not open her eyes by saying too much. In those days, by virtue of her position as a "little mother", in the sense given by the Convent to those words, she could still exercise some authority over her charge. She did her best to divert the child's ardent affections into the channels of the spirit. At first Gisèle followed her precepts so unquestioningly that Monsieur de Plailly took offence. Since the village had no regular priest, the girl assumed the duty of instructing the local children in the catechism and of visiting the sick. Things came to a head when, after reading a Life of Saint-Theresa she decided to become a Carmelite nun.

Her father was not then the old peasant grubbing in his kitchen garden and pilfering birds' eggs from their nests, that he afterwards became. But he had already made up his mind never to give Gisèle a dowry, and never to share her with anybody else. He accused Lucile of "putting ideas" into his daughter's head, and forbade her the house. "I ought" reflected Lucile, "to have put up a fight. It was wrong in me to abandon the young life which had been confided to my care, whose terrible destiny I already guessed." She never ceased to reproach herself with that defection, and even now, so long afterwards, was pronouncing sentence on herself as she sat in a railway carriage filled to bursting with human beings who, fundamentally, were not much different from the animals they bought and sold, with there, opposite, the sleeping Magdalene with a wisp of hair straying over her grubby cheek. A smell of wood-ash was blowing in through the open windows from the burned out conflagrations of Les Landes. Yes, she held herself bitterly to blame, and the sense of her guilt was sharpened by the presence at her side of the nuzzling Marie. She could smell that peculiar odour of sour milk that little girls give off on hot summer days.

"My sin in those days was that I thought only of myself." It had been the year when she had been under constant pressure from her parents and her brothers – who were older than she was – to marry Marc de Villeron. He was their principal shareholder, and the future of the mills depended on the marriage. She was conscious of no vocation for the cloister. The men of her family, northerners all, who regularly installed a figure of Christ or of the Virgins in their workrooms, would have acquiesced in her decision to take the veil. What she could not make them understand was that she had already become aware of a different sort of duty, that of hacking a passage for herself through the thickets of the world, and of setting up her habitation upon the very verges of the

River of Fire. They said she was proud: they said she was neurasthenic – and all because she had listened to a call beyond their comprehension. Villeron was a decent enough fellow, she knew that. But that knowledge did not prevent her from hating the sight of his hairy fingers when he poured himself a glass of brandy to keep the cold out: from hating the satisfied voice in which, while comfortably digesting his food, he solved the problems of his self-indulgent world while airily blaming three quarters of its inhabitants for all he found to dislike in it: from hating even his cigar, his powerful nickel-plated car, which was more like a two-seater projectile than a vehicle. She scoffed at his aping of Anglo-Saxon manners, at his loud, checked sports suits which accentuated his fat legs and protuberant paunch, and made him look ridiculous and horrible. Last of all, Christian though she was, she abominated, dared to abominate, his religious faith, which was no more than an item of personal hygiene, an insurance policy against the risks of a future life, on which he was careful to pay a premium to the interested party. But when she scrutinized her conscience she was far too clear-sighted not to detect all too large a dose of gall. She called herself to stand before the bar of truth, and passed an adverse sentence. When she agreed to marry Marc de Villeron, the members of her family not unnaturally felt that there had been a battle, and that

they had won it. Actually, the high-spirited young
woman had yielded only to her own felt need to do penitence. She was her own executioner, and in doing what
she did, accepted, with her eyes open, something which
she felt to be the worst of all possible fates.

But all through those struggles of contending wills,
had she not been guilty of neglecting the young creature
to whom she was so deeply attached? During all that
summer, Gisèle de Plailly had spent most of each day
lying on the flagstones of the terrace, with little on
beneath her shift, revelling in the feel of dry warmth
against her body, letting her left arm hang, like a sleeping
snake, over the wall that overhung the road along which
the young men of the village regularly passed. Then had
come the Autumn. The winds blowing across the empty
plain spoiled the chemical manure: the beet-pulp rotted
in the silos: the torn and twisted branches of the beech
trees covered the garden in deep drifts of ravelled, yellow
leaves. It was then that Gisèle de Plailly, squatting before
the fire, had looked for and found in books the explanation of her bodily distress; had come, in Littré and the
Encyclopaedia, on detailed articles illustrated with sug-
gestive, terrifying plates.

For two years Lucile was a model wife, concealing her
face behind a smiling mask. Then the war came. Marc
de Villeron, who had been badly bowled over by the

destruction of many mines and factories with which his
fortune was involved, was struck down by apoplexy on
the very day that a Medical Board passed him fit for
active service. It was then that his widow realized the
depravity of her heart. Two of her brothers had been
killed, and all her folk were plunged in desperate misery.
But her only feeling was one of frenzied joy such as one
buried alive might know when the imprisoning tomb
is rent by some remorseless cataclysm. She worried
very little, if at all, about Gisèle. The first thing she did
was to take an apartment in the rue Vaneau. Later, she got
herself attached to a surgical unit at Toul. One evening
in March she happened to travel to Paris in order to take
delivery of a consignment of instruments. She quickly
climbed the stairs which were plunged in darkness owing
to the threat of raiding Gothas. Just as she was opening
her own front door, her eye caught a crouching human
figure. She bent down, recognized the woman at her feet,
raised her in her arms, carried her into the flat and laid
her down upon a bed. She took off her boots and stood
silently waiting for Gisèle to say something. But the girl
made it clear by signs that she could not speak. . . Lucile
could do nothing but repeat, over and over again, as
though the words she uttered were a hymn of praise –
"this day of all days, just when I happened to be passing
through Paris!" She comforted the girl. Monsieur de

Plailly should be made to believe that Gisèle had dis-
obeyed him, and had joined her friend in the Field Hospital. "Your child shall be my child, our child." And
then she said again what she had already said – "to think
that it should have been this day of all days!" The memory of that night was sweet to her. She had sat beside the
bed, rocking Gisèle's poor outraged body into sleep,
while above the black crater of Paris, aeroplanes had
droned across the sky. How lovely that night had been,
compared with the one now ended only a few hours ago.
Oh God! – not yet twenty-four hours! Could this new
horror be so close as that? Gisèle's absence, the terrible
silence of the next-door room, had wakened her. She
had got up, choked back a cry at sight of the empty bed,
then, pausing only to throw a coat about her shoulders,
had hastened down the corridor to where a motionless
and fearful light was showing from under Daniel Trasis's
double doors. She could not tell how long she had stood
with her eyes upon those doors, her ears alive to the sighs
and groans of questing bodies, powerless, crucified against
the wall. A moth thumped against the glass of the dim
night lamp. Somebody in the next room was snoring,
choking, struggling for breath. Pairs of shapeless shoes
dotted the corridor. Far away she could hear the grating
song of cicadas in the summer night.

They must be nearing Bordeaux, because a woman

who, a while back, had smiled apologies ("this heat makes the feet swell so") was buttoning up her boots with the help of a hairpin. Lucile had to guide a whimpering Marie towards the lavatory. The child staggered down the crowded corridor, bumping into legs as though they had been so many trees. When at last, they reached the lavatory, she was overcome by terror at the rattling of the windows and the banging jolts, so that Lucile had to support her small body on the seat. When they got back, Gisèle had woken up and was showing signs of uneasiness at their absence. Without so much as glancing at her friend, she took Marie for a moment on her lap, then, pushing her away, went into the corridor and stood with her face pressed to the window. A breeze from the empty spaces blew in her hair. "What is she thinking of," Lucile wondered. She knew that women can plunge again into the River of Fire even when he who thrust them there is no longer present in the flesh. The River of Fire is within us. It was in Gisèle now, with the wounds of love's caresses still a living memory, more burning hot than physical scars; a poisoned memory.

Gisèle de Plailly wanted to think about Daniel. But as when two exposures have been made on the same photographic plate, his features were blurred by those of another . . . Trained in the meticulous examination of her conscience, she was thinking back to the moment of her

fall, and saw two faces, one living, and one dead. The
documents in the case by now were all confused, the old
extenuating circumstances no longer available for use.
What she was remembering were the last days of her
girlhood's innocence, her father's fits of anger and moods
of panic because the back area troops had invaded his
home, because the soldiers were taking the handles off
the doors, throwing rubbish into the cesspool, stealing
the chickens and the fruit. It was in these days that she
had begun to go hungry, and at night, would lie in bed
with chattering teeth when the sound of aeroplanes
awakened her, and the rumbling of motor convoys moving up towards the front. Every now and again, an enormous searchlight, sweeping round the sky, would invade
the privacy of her room and dazzle her with a momentary glare. On the stairs, two corpulent officers of the
Supply Services, would salute as she passed, and then
stare gluttonously after her disappearing figure. She had
been forbidden by her father to set foot in a military hospital, and the only thing left for her to do was to wander
about Paris, unoccupied, famished, and cut off from God.

For God no longer had His habitation in the church
where now, at night, the visiting birds dirtied the altar
with their droppings. The children used it for their games,
hiding in the pulpit, and pulling out the organ stops.
When darkness fell, and the nearby A.A. battery opened

fire, the falling shrapnel bullets would patter on the roof tiles, and force old Plailly to take refuge in the cellar. There he would sit behind the furnace, clutching on his skinny knees a brief case stuffed with Russian Bonds, and saying over and over again, like a child, that they must "clear out", that he had had as much as he could stand. But when morning brought comfort, nothing in the world would induce him to abandon his property. Besides, where could they have found anywhere to live? Then, with her string bag in her hand, in the freezing dawn or the falling rain, she would wait for the coming of the 'bus. She had persuaded her father that food cost less in Paris, and that by doing her marketing there she could more than make up the cost of a third-class return fare. So it was that she became one tiny drop in the black wave of humanity which the Gare du Nord spewed out upon the pavements. Released for a while from prison, she breathed more freely. It was as though her weariness and misery had become absorbed into, lost in, the flood that filled the streets. She was sucked into the Underground, forced onwards like a subterranean river, and disgorged with the crowd through one or other of its hundred mouths, and herded into the dark caverns of the picture theatres.

In those years of wretchedness and madness, in her aimless wanderings about the city, she never openly admitted to herself that she was waiting for, hoping for, some chance meeting, some momentary consolation in the darkness where the awareness of furtive love-making assailed her on all sides. Indeed, when night came, and the moment of her journey home, she would sit in her unlighted railway carriage, one of a suburban crowd, sighing with relief that nothing had happened. Little by little she actually acquired a melancholy sense of safety, a conviction that, in spite of herself, she was being protected. It was, she felt, beyond her power to fall: something was forbidding her to sin. She would walk miraculously upon the waters.

It was then that, lured into imprudence, and without fully realizing what she was doing, she came to give her wanderings a quality of active searching. Not that by look or gesture did she invite casual encounters. It was just that she moved about the city with a heightened awareness of every young face that passed her, and of the expression in strange eyes. Her sense of security increased merely because for a long while she resisted the proffered suggestions of the streets. It was never those whom, perhaps, she might have been following who turned to accost her. More than once, in the Underground or the suburban train, feeling the insistent gaze of some young man upon her, she would say to herself, "if he speaks to me" . . . but always the unknown admirer got out at some

H

station that was not her own. She became convinced that
the Everlasting Mercy had condemned her to attract
only the most repulsive specimens of the male. When
she heard behind her the footsteps of a hot pursuit, she
would hesitate before turning her head, so that for just
one more minute she might enjoy the thought that this
time she would really see the sunburned face of which
she had dreamed. But, when turn she did, it was always
to find herself in the presence of a breathless man of fifty.

How heavy weighed her adamantine armour! How
eagerly she longed to be abandoned, weaponless, ex-
posed! Once more the Spring came round, heavy with
panic, and once more the villagers fled from their homes.
Each night now, beyond the garden, guns barked at the
sky, and Monsieur de Plailly, half mad, chattered to himself in the cellar. The dawn brought her freedom, but
the evening led her home with bleeding feet, and dead
with all the hungers of the flesh.

One afternoon, she came to anchor in a cinema on the
Avenue Wagram. The human atmosphere and the music
opened to let her in, then closed behind her, warm, welcoming, rich with the promise of forgetfulness. The seat
next to hers was empty. Who, she thought to herself,
will sit in it? probably some fat man, or some woman,
as usual. But he who came this time was an Officer Cadet.
Even before she saw his clear cut profile, his baby eye-

lashes, his hollow cheeks, she could smell the leather
polish on his belt. The house was rocking with laughter,
and he alone was grave, as though the screen on which
Charlie Chaplin splashed through the trenches, was re-
minding him of what lay in wait for him some six days
hence. Her knee touched his, as though by accident, and
he returned the pressure, perhaps just to discover whether
she had made that contact of set purpose. They sat for a
while like that, hesitating. Another film was shown –
featuring love and orgy in the clubs of New York. The
violins and the 'cellos wailed in excruciating delight to
the strains of *Werther* and *'Allo Chéri*. The young sol-
dier's knee beat out the rhythm, finding a willing partner
in her own. She remembered that moment of ashamed
surrender: she remembered their wordless understanding,
her furtive entry into an hotel on the Place des Ternes,
while she wished that she were dead. Then she remembered Daniel, and the way, only twenty-four hours ago,
in which she had followed him into his room. "I only
meant to push a letter under his door . . . but wasn't I
really hoping that he would understand what I was after?
Of course I was! . . . There was no need for me to push
it under his door. I could have left it at the desk." How
could she possibly excuse such shamelessness? What was
her first fall from virtue compared with this terrible relapse? How venial seemed her earlier weakness in the light

of this delicious crime of the night just passed. The Cadet's family lived at Mulhouse, and he had crossed the frontier leaving his relations there. He knew nobody in Paris except a "pen-friend" of the war, a woman who had developed a great contempt of him ever since he had foolishly confessed how, in his first action, he had "gone to ground" in a shell-hole. Tearful sin is different from sin in joy. The boy whom she had casually picked up had nothing in common with those brave warriors of whom it was the fashion of the times to say that they "were longing to get back to the front". On that last afternoon in the squalid room on the Place des Ternes, his kisses had been those of a child, and they were the only ones that she had truly loved. She could still feel between her shoulder and her neck, the bristly cheek wet with tears. "Those were the only kisses of his that I really loved." Nothing had moved her as they had done, except the feel of his knee against hers in the darkened cinema. Then, ah then, her weary heart had pounded so violently that she had found it difficult to breathe . . . Only when they had left the theatre, and were standing on the pavement of the Avenue Wagram, had she seen his worn and menaced face in the transparent dusk. How desperately at that moment she had longed to run away! Later, when she rehearsed the circumstances of her fall, she had taken all the blame upon herself. She had forced herself to yield, had searched out death and willed it. It was only at the cost of a great effort, by overcoming her own resistance, that she had managed to achieve that act of falling. All defences had gone down before her longing to rid herself of the heavy armour of virtue, to break the ring of the encircling angels, to dig within the substance of her life, the great abyss of an irremediable decision. How well she remembered the short journey to the Place des Ternes. He had walked ahead, turning from time to time, to smile at her. The blue garter round her left leg had worked a little loose. She recalled how, when she had left the room and had sat in the Underground on her way to the Gare du Nord, she had shut her eyes and tried to empty her face of all expression because it had nothing to show but horror and fear. But her mouth, though she did not know it, had been eloquent of disgust. And yet, through five whole days she had gone back . . . He had so little time . . . For knowledge of death was in his eyes and in his silences. When he talked about planning for the future, it betrayed itself in a certain movement of his hands and shoulders. "I know that I loved him . . ." Destiny had brought her the gift of that one face, and greedily she had seized on it. We love where we can. As a child who has no toys makes a doll from rags, so does the heart's ingenuity compound from Fate's niggardly generosity, a thing to love. So, she wiped from her face all that did not serve the purposes of love, and, like a tendril of ivy, clung to the only body she could find. That same face, young and ill-shaved, had looked so miserable when they stood together outside the cinema. When she saw it on the departure platform it was as her heart had reconstructed it, thin to emaciation, all spirit, the nose so finely drawn that even death would never need to pinch it more, and life brooding – but for how long? – in the deep-set eyes. She had seen the last of him on that station platform, and had felt almost indifferent, since there was nothing she could do to save him. No, sinning with laughter, and sinning in tears, are two quite different things. He must have been killed very soon after that farewell, for all her letters were sent back to her, except the first.

She heard Marie crying, and went back into the carriage. The child was whimpering something about having got a piece of coal-dust in her eye . . . Madame de Villeron was saying that she would bathe the eye as soon as they could get to the station buffet. But Gisèle could not bear to see the child in pain. She took her on her knee, and tried to raise the lid. But Marie struggled and screamed.

"Try your wedding ring, Madame," advised the lady who had just put on her boots again. Gisèle blushed, took the gold ring which Lucile handed her, and touched the cornea with it, but to no purpose. The other occupants of the carriage started telling stories of persons they had known who had got pieces of coal-dust in their eyes. That sort of thing could be very serious. She really ought to ask one of the railway officials for the name of an oculist. At last the child, as a result of crying so much worked the cinder out of her eye. All the same, when they got to the buffet, she still complained of having a headache, and as soon as the Paris train was made up, Gisèle got her to lie down on the seat of a first-class carriage, where she soon shut her eyes and went to sleep. The anxious mother lightly touched her forehead and her neck.

"She seems rather hot to me", she murmured, "see what you think, Lucile . . ."

Madame de Villeron, in her turn, laid her hand on Marie's eyes, and took the skinny little wrist between her fingers.

"Nonsense, she's as cool as . . ."

"As a hanging peach . . ." Gisèle completed the sentence with a smile, because she knew her friend's liking for the image.

Lucile saw hope in this sign of slackening tension. When the train started before anybody else had invaded the carriage, she took her courage in both hands:

"How you do love that child of yours, Gisèle . . ."

The sinner's brow contracted in a frown. "I've had enough of that sort of blackmailing . . ." she said in a low voice, and the look she gave Marie was almost one of hatred.

Madame de Villeron blamed herself for having spoken too soon. Gisèle had completely lost control of herself.

"I know that it's through the child that you keep a hold on me . . . I can't help knowing it . . . She's much more yours than mine . . . I've long ceased to have any part in her."

Now that she had started, she went on and on . . . her pent up feelings poured out in a flood of disconnected phrases.

"I'm nothing to you but an occasion for one of your good deeds. . . . You don't begin to understand me. There are some things of which you have no conception" (again that grating laugh rang out). "I remember you telling me once that you had asked your husband whether there wasn't some other way of having babies."

She tried again to force a laugh, but could not. The very coarseness of the words, however, had the effect of calming her down almost as soon as she had uttered them. The train rushed through some nameless station with a bang and a rattle. Lucile said nothing in reply, but pulled the rug up over the restless child.

"Speak lower", she said, "she might hear you." Then she dimmed the light and leaned back in her corner. Her

face froze into a mask of death. Only her lips moved in
silent prayer. Her right hand was tightly clenched on the
black beads of her rosary. The radiance of that worn and
weary face, so seamed with tears, was more than Gisèle
could bear. How she hated Lucile's passion for dragging
her from the River! What a mania the woman had for
saving those who longed to be lost! All she wanted was
to find Daniel again; to drown; to overwhelm her self-
appointed guardian in the waters of disgust. But was that
possible? It was not enough that she was incapable of sin:
she was no less incapable, as Gisèle well knew, of any
feeling of contempt, being obsessed by the Saviour's
peculiar liking for lost sheep. Her power over this sinner,
and over others too, sprang largely from the fact that she
could always convince the fallen that they were the re-
cipients of some mysterious favour. When she had taken
Marie in, and Gisèle had gone back to her family, Madame
de Villeron had sent her daily letters. The gist of each was
that the Gospel is in part the story of the hungry and the
thirsty who have been turned from the pleasures of mortal sin to seek the waters of life. That being so, she would
write, the very craving which had led them to be damned,
was turned into the means of their salvation. Was not
that passion for self-destruction which can be found in
passion at its most intense, that utter surrender to sin,
sometimes the sign of a vocation? She had repeated that

over and over again to the fallen girl, and Gisèle, still extraordinarily childish for her age, had soon come again
under Lucile's influence. On the fly-leaf of a secret note-
book, she had written in an unformed hand – just as
though she were still at the Convent, the words: *Some
Thoughts of L. de V., together with extracts from her Letters.*
Isolated from their context, these maxims culled from
the wisdom of a saintly woman, might well have given
rise to scandal. Gisèle smiled wryly when she remembered
some of the sentences that she had noted down: *It is only
the hungers of mankind that our Saviour loves:* and, *The Saviour never told human beings that they should follow the ex-
ample of the Angels: an Angel is the least admirable of Beings.*
Lucile de Villeron had, indeed, carried self-contempt to
extremes, and would never seek to glorify her own an-
gelic qualities. Her religious ardour crystallized about the
lost piece of silver, and that image of the Prodigal who,
on returning home, hot from the arms of harlots, was
loved more dearly than his elder brother.

Gisèle sat studying the face of her sleeping companion.
How could she break from her once and for all, how
could she drive her from the banks of the River of Fire,
and make her abandon one whose only wish was to be
consumed? She lowered one of the windows. The faithful moon was keeping pace with the express, turning the
world to a milky whiteness, laying a loving touch upon

the long, straight roads. Daniel, Daniel, Daniel! The sky over Argelès, over the grassy banks beside the waterfall, over Mont Pibeste and the Saint-Savin road, must at this very moment be drenched in the self-same radiance. Only last night this very moon had forced two bodies, close held in the conspiracy of love, to see each other clearly in that culminating point of passion which should pass in darkness. Gisèle stretched her hand into the night. Her mind was filled entirely with the thought of Daniel. At no matter what cost she must see him again. As though this were the very moment of her flight she gazed upon her sleeping guardian in silent farewell. Then, suddenly, that other guardian, her own small daughter, woke in a fright, and Gisèle took her on her knee, and rocked her gently till the child's head nodded into sleep, and she could lay her down again upon the seat. Then, as a dog digs up a buried bone, she sought again the memory of Daniel, and slaked her thirst with dreaming. Daniel! Daniel! – she would find him again, that she never doubted, but how would he receive her? He had been hard, had as good as driven her away . . . but that had been because he feared that Lucile might be outside the door. "I'm sure he's missing me, now at this very moment." Desire for her was waking in his flesh. By this time he must have read her letter. But suppose he drove her away again? True enough, she had deceived him, for had he not told her that he had loved an unspotted girl who had no real existence? The manias of men are beyond understanding. That other, too, on their last day together, had pleaded that she should be an elder sister to him. There is never any knowing what the debauched really want!... Daniel! Daniel! – no doubt about it, *he* was debauched – and Gisèle, caught in a memory, trembled. "It is almost as though men seek in us their own lost innocence . . ."

Day broke. It was almost cold, and Gisèle de Plailly closed the window. "Yesterday, at this very hour . . ." she murmured. To force an entry into Daniel's life would be no more possible than to cast Lucile or Marie out of her own. What being, what world, can break free of its constellation? But she would let nothing stop her from pursuing him. She would torment and harry him. "Do I, then, love him that much?" True, she had not sought him out; he had flashed into her ken like a falling star. Would not someone else have done just as well? So violent was her feeling of disgust that her mouth drooped at the corners. But not for nothing had she been Lucile's pupil. From her she had learned the terrible technique of self scrutiny which so few have the courage to employ, the piercing look into the heart, the Catholic look.

She had never told herself that she had "a right to love" nor had ever flattered herself, as she passed from man to man, that she was seeking the ideal attachment. With an all too lucid eye she had measured the depth of the pit into which she had fallen.

She emerged from the depths of her meditation, looked for a moment at the sleeping Lucile, then moved close to her as though seeking protection from her thoughts. The carriage windows dirtied the light of the new day. Lacking the courage to remain alone with her own heart, she touched her friend's clasped hands. Lucile awoke with a start.

"What's the matter?"

"I'm hungry."

Madame de Villeron took some bread and a bar of chocolate from her travelling bag. She watched Gisèle eat. The girl's face under her tousled hair was pale. Her rather heavy jaw bit into the bread with the voraciousness of an animal, and all the while her fixed, her almost dead, stare never once moved from the point in space on which it seemed to be fixed. For a moment Lucile remained plunged in thought: then she interrupted her morning prayer to say:

"I suppose you realize that I am taking you with me?"

Gisèle made no protest, but merely asked:

"To Dunkirk?"

"Naturally . . . Your father gave you leave of absence for a month. We still have twelve days left."

The girl answered with a gesture of resignation, and Lucile was just on the point of silently thanking God, when her young friend suddenly mastered her momentary mood of apathy.

"No," she exclaimed, "no – that's impossible." It had come to her in a flash that Daniel would be bound to write to her at the address she had given him. It was essential that she should be in a position to run to him at the first summons. Not for anything in the world would she consent to move from the immediate neighbourhood of Paris. The reasons, however, which she gave for her determination were not the true ones. She was afraid, she said, that Lucile's mother and brothers might guess her shame.

"That's nonsense! They think I adopted a war orphan. It would never occur to them to imagine . . ."

"But others, as you very well know, have guessed it . . ." This allusion to Daniel made both of them blush. Lucile, with her eyes averted, said:

"That's quite different."

Gisèle turned away her head. The platforms of the small stations through which they were now running were thronged with workers waiting for the suburban trains. Austerlitz could not be far off. Only a few moments were left in which Madame de Villeron could break down her friend's resistance. She tried to imagine the nature of the obstacle, felt sure that she was on the right track, and burst out irritably:

"The fact is you don't want to be away from Paris..."

"If I don't, it's not for the reason you think."

Gisèle repeated her first objection, adding that her father would be furious if she went to Dunkirk. She seemed quite calm, almost listless. But she was determined not to yield. From now on, her whole existence must be conditioned to waiting – to waiting for Daniel's letter. There were two posts a day in the village where she lived – enough to fill her life. Very quietly, she said:

"Don't try to persuade me . . ."

Did Lucile really think that one could so easily turn one's back on the "second time?" She did not realize how unlikely it was that a man should, of his own free will, refuse a renewal of what had brought him so much joy.

The mere possibility that Daniel might take steps to get in touch with her sufficed to restore Gisèle to her natural self. She set about dabbing at Marie with Eau de Cologne, after which she renewed her own make-up, reddening her lips and covering the grime of the night with powder. Lucile watched the poor bird smoothing its dishevelled plumage. The train was already moving out of the Austerlitz station. Suddenly Madame de Villeron said, almost casually:

"On second thoughts, I don't think I shall go back to Dunkirk."

Gisèle, who was taking the bags down from the rack, swung round, prepared to give battle:

"I hope you're not proposing to come home with me? You won't get a very warm welcome, you know."

Madame de Villeron protested that no such idea had ever entered her mind. It was only that her friend, Emma Buffaut, had organized a sewing-party at Versailles, and had been at her for months to give a hand. She'd got no plans for the second half of the month, and the opportunity was too good to be missed. The air of Versailles would be just the thing for Marie. Gisèle gave a nervous laugh:

"You must please yourself", she said: and then, again, "You must please yourself." She knew that no watchful eyes could keep that letter from reaching her, that nothing and nobody would be strong enough to separate her from the man who was her master.

"Perhaps you could come and see Marie at Versailles?"

At that moment the train ran into the terminus, and Gisèle made no reply. She hurried to the exit. Lucile followed carrying a bag and pulling Marie after her. When at last she came up with her friend on the Quai d'Orsay, the latter said:

"Is it your intention to come with me to the Gare du Nord?"

"Yes, Gisèle."

They hailed a taxi. Not a word did they exchange during the drive. Lucile settled the girl in the train for Creil.

"You're not, surely, going to wait until we start?"

"Yes, Gisèle, I am" – then, dropping her voice "you will come and see Marie at Versailles, won't you?"

Mademoiselle de Plailly said nothing. She took the child in her arms for a moment, then settled back into her seat, opened a magazine, and did not so much as raise her eyes until the train shuddered into motion. She saw her guardian standing motionless on precisely the same spot as before, her hat awry, her skirt stained with dust. Marie, a weak and sickly figure at her side, was waving a hand.

IV

A S the first drops from a stormy rain-cloud starred the terrace steps, Lucile uttered her uneasiness aloud. In a low voice, she said: "and the child's not back yet". She got up from her chair and went to the window. Beyond the tiny garden the trees in the Avenue de Villeneuve-l'Étang were already losing their leaves. Marie's nurse was on holiday in Dublin, and until she returned Lucile hated to be parted from the child. She blamed herself for having handed her over to the tender mercies of the "general", a woman of whom she knew nothing, for the duration of their stay at Versailles. But Marie must have fresh air, and she, Lucile, could not, would not, leave the house. "If I were away even for an hour, Gisèle would be sure to choose that moment to come, and I must be here to open the door . . ." For a whole week now she had been living the life of a prisoner, listening to the sound of every footstep . . . Nobody had been to see her except her friend Emma Buffaut, and from *her* visits she had derived more of boredom than of comfort. The days were too short to exhaust her burning thoughts, her flow of prayers, the inexhaustible stream of supplication to which she gave herself. She even neglected her correspondence, though she knew that to many her letters were as necessary as daily bread. Anybody else would have succumbed under the weight of hours spent in a house which she had taken by the month, condemned to look at portraits and photographs which meant nothing to her – nameless faces, unknown life stories, shabby furniture, a lamp which lighted the hours of her long vigil, a book lying forgotten on a table. But Lucile de Villeron seemed to have eyes only for what lay within. She knew no reality save that of the inner life. It was as though she carried about with her the bare walls of a cell on which was nothing that might distract attention from the soul. On the mantelpiece stood an Empire clock with a pendulum which represented Time in the figure of an old man with a scythe. Marie worked away at her reading with solemn application, looking at the pictures in her books of Bible stories, tracing with a childish finger the spirals of an uncompleted Tower of Babel. When the evening was filled with rain she pressed her freckled face to the pane, breathing upon the glass – a child broken in to the discipline of silence. When she turned her head she saw "Mémé" seated motionless in her wicker chair, her clasped hands showing bright against the dark material of her dress. She would butt against them with her head, forcing them apart, compelling them to stroke her hair.

The solid rain was driving the withered leaves before

it. "The child's not back yet." Had she taken her mack-
intosh? A mother would have thought of that. "I've not
got enough of the mother in me . . . If Gisèle were to
come in now she would blame me. When she does
come . . ." – Lucile de Villeron did not doubt that Gisèle
would return to her – but after what new miseries? She
weighed the chances of a fresh relapse. How much trust
could she place in Daniel Trasis? She forced herself to
judge by what she knew of him. How she hated that tall
young man with the hungry eyes, the very image of
youthful vigour, a lean wolf, a male! But so extreme
was her scrupulousness that the very violence of her hostility filled her with uneasiness. Every night she drove
herself to pray for him. "I must love him, Lord: make
me love him, since such is Thy Will . . ." She could not
help remembering with a sense of horror the way he had
talked, the way he had moved, the way he had smelled
of Eau de Cologne and tobacco, the look of his heavy
jaw as she had seen it when she had surprised him in
Gisèle's room. Had her concern for him been nothing,
after all, but make-believe? No. For one thing, she felt
a deep compassion for all flesh, but more than that was
involved in her present state of mind. In the last few days
this particular miserable sinner had taken a cunning revenge on her. Precisely why her sense of pity had been
touched she could not have explained in words. It was

true, however, that this casual acquaintance had cast some kind of spell upon the icy waters of her tenderness. At early morning Mass – which she heard in a new brick church – she managed to recover her peace of mind, though, at the approach of evening, she lost it again. Something she said in a letter which she wrote about this time to a typist whom she had been instrumental in saving (the girl had thought herself beyond salvation) betrayed the secret of her deep uneasiness: "It may well be that no one in this world is wholly pure in heart. Absolute purity is an impossible state for human beings. Here, on this earth there is room only for sinners and those who have been cleansed of sin . . ." Doubtless she thought not worth consideration those men and women who are so little troubled by the stirrings of the flesh that we say of them "they just don't know what that sort of thing is like" – for she added – "Woe to those who take pride in not succumbing to temptations which they never feel." That was a comment she never tired of making, turning the words against herself because she, who hated the flesh, dreaded lest she find cause for pride in that very hatred. When of an evening in that house on the Avenue de Villeneuve-l'Étang, the child Marie hung about the woman who sat motionless with hands clasped on her sober-coloured gown, only God could tell whether Lucile de Villeron, turning her heart as a man might turn the desert sand with a plough, would not suddenly come on a seed, which, though she did not know it, had been working deep down in her from all eternity. If God knew, it was not His will that she should ever find it, nor that her heart, freed from the trammels of Evil, should ever be profoundly troubled.

She was to remember later, that day of storm and waiting. It had produced in her a mood of fear which her reason could not explain. Since the day of her First Communion, she had felt life as a continual eagerness. She would never admit any limits to purity or perfection, and knew that in the endless upward climb it was dangerous to leave the spirit, even for a moment, in suspense. She went back again to the window. She could hear nothing but the rain pattering on the leaves, the gurgling of water in the gutters, and far away, the grinding wheels and clanging bell of a tram in the rue Duplessis – It occurred to her that the child might be lost. How ridiculous! She shook her head, smiled, and murmured to herself: "I would never have believed I could have got so fond of her! . . ." And yet, that same child was Gisèle's sin incarnate, the living proof of her incurable weakness, error that lived and breathed in one small body . . . "That only makes me love her the more . . . I don't believe I could ever have felt the same devotion to a child born of a happy marriage." Whether this love of hers was

according to God's will, she did not know. She smiled
because, in the mirror of her heart, she could see reflected
Marie's innocent eyes, Marie's freckled face, Marie's untroubled thoughts. The purity of childhood! – *Become as
little children* . . . "Have I become like Marie?" She turned
her gaze inwards, sought the place where dwelt her one
and only love, and with eyes closed, pronounced the
adored, the sacred Name. Her poverty of spirit blew
on dead ashes, and dropped exhausted. But with this
sluggishness of soul there now chimed the sensation of
her swift-flowing blood. It filled her with a mysterious
well-being, with a new, a troubled happiness in which
the movement of her will had no part. She was conscious in her innermost being of numbness lifted ... Self-
knowledge is hidden from those who live always in
obedience to a rule that cannot be broken, for they know
nothing of the paths that lead into the depths. She exam-
ined her conscience and found little enough for reproach
– at most some small negligence touching her relations
with her spiritual director. He had long blamed in her
an excess of confidence, a too great love of daring. She
relied, he said, too much on her own strength of mind.
True it was that never before tonight had she shown such
weakness, found such sweetness in the taste of tears, or
felt, in so acute a form, the longing for human consolation. On what, on whom, did she crave to rest her head,

and why did her hands lie open on her lap – expectant of what alms?

She heard beneath the sound of the falling rain Marie's hurrying footsteps, and Marie's voice calling to her. The child had left the garden door open.

"Mémé, guess who's here, guess who's come!" Madame de Villeron flung the window wide and, in spite of the rain, leaned out. A name had risen to her lips, but she dared not speak it. Marie, her hood about her face, had stopped on the threshold. Her head was turned towards the new arrival. Gisèle appeared under a streaming umbrella. Marie, running ahead, burst into the room crying:

"Here's Aunt Gisèle!"

Lucile went to give the child a welcoming kiss, and found her taking off her overshoes in the hall.

"How wet you are, my pet. I'll tell the girl to dry your coat in the kitchen."

"Isn't it good news?"

"It certainly isn't bad news, but I don't quite know what to say . . . you see, I hadn't planned to take her to Dunkirk. Wouldn't you like something hot to drink, Gisèle?"

Mademoiselle de Plailly shook her head, tidied her hair, and followed Lucile into the drawing-room. She opened her bag.

"I've brought some sweeties for you, Marie." They

sat down side by side in the darkest corner of the room, on the Second-Empire couch with its torn covering of cherry-coloured silk.

"What a day! Luckily I found the tram waiting at the station."

"Why didn't you write?"

"I just didn't know which way to turn . . . and, if it comes to that, *you* didn't write to *me* . . ."

She explained that the servant had had a bad attack of rheumatism:

"And so, you see, I had to do everything."

She spoke of the washing, of the chickens, but said nothing about her father, which was very unlike her. On and on she jabbered just for the sake of keeping more serious matters at bay. At last she could find nothing more to say . . . They could hear the ticking of the clock, and each the muted throbbing of her blood. Lucile de Villeron looked at the other's heavy laced boots and black woollen dress. One of Gisèle's hands was concealed in a darned thread glove: the other was bare and lay upon the couch. Its nails were worn and broken as a result of heavy work. Lucile could not see the face, which was half-turned from her in shame. She tried to take the uncovered hand in hers, but it was at once withdrawn.

"Gisèle!"

In a very low voice (because Marie, by the window,

was emptying the bag of sweets into a box), the girl said:

"I was too frightened to come."

This time Lucile managed to take the hand. There was no attempt at escape. She said:

"Marie, my pet, run away and play."

But the child had crept close to Gisèle who kept her from moving, holding her against her body like a shield, as though she were hoping that the presence of her there would prevent the necessity of discussing with Lucile things that were over and done with. She hoped that in the gloom, Marie would not see the traces of tears upon her cheeks. She had not expected the child to put her lips to her face.

"Mémé, Aunt Gisèle is crying!"

Though that plaintive little cry had set the tears flowing again, Mademoiselle de Plailly tried to control herself in the child's presence. She was sitting very upright, very stiffly, but her body was trembling like a leaf. She said:

"No, Marie, no, I'm not crying . . ." but the little girl insisted.

"Yes, you are – my fingers are all wet!"

Madame de Villeron told her that her aunt was unhappy because her father was ill. She mustn't bother her. It had stopped raining now . . . she could go and play in the garden.

As soon as Marie had left the room, she went back to her sobbing visitor who now sat doubled up, her face almost touching her knees. "Gisèle!" she said again, but got no answer. She put a question in a low voice:

"Have you seen him again?"

The young woman sat up suddenly:

"Oh no!" she exclaimed, "no – I swear I haven't!"

"Well, then . . ."

Lucile spoke conventional words of comfort and confidence. Her voice sounded flat. Coldness had suddenly succeeded to her warmth. Gisèle's tears had ceased to flow. The expression of her face was fixed and thoughtful. She broke in upon her friend.

"I haven't seen him . . . perhaps because he hasn't asked me to. Don't run away with the idea that I have changed. I think that if, on that first day, he had asked me to go back to him, I should have gone. I'm not absolutely certain, but I think I should . . ."

She spoke slowly, deliberately. She looked into her heart, and, anxious to tell the truth, scrupulous for exactitude, confessed what she had found there. Lucile refrained from uttering a word. It was not for her to interrupt Gisèle who was soaring at so great a height, who, all of a sudden, had flown beyond her reach. It was she now, Lucile, she now, the saint, who felt her

heart troubled, heavy and untouched by joy at so mani-
fest a case of resurrection.

"When I left you", Gisèle was saying, "I had only one
thought – to turn again to my sinning, and, by every
trick in my power, to avoid your watchful care. I waited
for him to give me a sign . . . What my nights were like
you can have no conception. But, with every day that
passed, I began to suffer a little bit less from his silence . . .
Then, a moment came when I actually feared that he
might turn up, but now even that dread has almost vanished. What I am describing to you was not my doing:
my own will played no part in it . . . it was as though
someone else had taken my place . . . How can I make
you understand? The beast howling its hunger in my
heart fell silent, and another voice which I had long
ceased to hear, sounded in my ears. Lucile, you're not
listening!"

Madame de Villeron made a movement of protest.
Without looking at her friend she murmured:

"I must have been mad, yes, mad, to leave you like
that to your own devices, to do no more for you than
watch and pray. Was I not tempting God? He has spared
you in His mercy, but I – I should have kept you with
me, even, if necessary, by force!"

She spoke these last words in a voice so harsh with
bitterness, that Gisèle raised her eyes. But the room at

this late hour of the rainy afternoon was almost dark, and she could see nothing but a calm, impassive face. Greatly daring, she said:

"That is very far from the truth. You were, in fact, most blessedly inspired. Your prayers saved me far more effectively than your presence could have done."

A few moments passed in complete silence, for each of them was occupied with deep and secret thoughts.

"Be frank, Gisèle: that day at the Gare du Nord, when the train began to move and you saw the last of me, your only feeling was relief ... you can't deny that, can you?"

She put the question with so detached, so indifferent an air that the younger woman was deceived.

"You really are an amazing person, Lucile! I can say anything to you: you are so far above petty human susceptibilities ... like a confessor. What other real confessor have I ever had than you? That is what gives you your power. Listen to what I am going to say ... but don't be angry ... you won't, will you?"

The other slowly raised her two hands, took her friend's face between them, and, with a sort of violent gentleness compelled it to look at her.

"When have I ever been angry with my little daughter?"

Giséle freed herself, and said:

"There's no reason for you to feel hurt at what I'm

going to say. After all, you understood my state of mind
so well that you kept from writing to me. How profound
your knowledge of the human soul is! It wasn't your
fault if the way you protected and watched over me at
Argelès made me irritable and exasperated. You remember how furious I was during that horrible drive to the
Gare du Nord, and you guessed why it was. As soon as
I had parted from you I felt almost calm . . ."

This time a note of anguish sounded in Lucile's voice
as she put a question:

"You don't mean that if I *hadn't* been with you there
at Argelès . . .?"

"Oh no, Lucile – no . . . Besides, who can say now
what might or might not have happened? You have often
told me that even God Himself cannot change the past.
Don't misunderstand me. I was furious because you had
spoken to . . ."

She could not bring herself to call Daniel Trasis by his
name, but deep within herself she heard it sound. In the
pause that followed, Madame de Villeron said in a voice
so low that it was almost a whisper:

"You see, I knew you so well, my poor darling . . .
knew that if you surrendered, it was because the same
hunger which long ago had brought about your fall, was
with you still. If you have not gone back to him, the
chief reason is, no doubt, that he has not given you a

sign, though I hope, too, that though I was absent from you in the flesh, my prayers, my suffering played a part. But something else, something purely human, must have contributed to your victory, something that had nothing to do with his silence and my absence. Look into your heart, darling. Why did you not go to him? Isn't the answer that he had deceived you? Come now, admit it . . . surely you can tell me?"

To judge from her voice, her face at that moment must have expressed a great hunger and a great desolation.

Gisèle de Plailly bowed her head still further. "It is so impossible to find the right words" she said. "Frankly, I don't know what I felt, except that he had *not* deceived me . . . You see, I had never really expected anything else . . . Listen, Lucile: you are perfectly right; I can tell you everything. I think that the power which was granted me to resist the desire I felt to go back to him, has been with me ever since that time at Argelès. No, don't protest. I had stood up to him, even before you arrived. Actually, I had begged him to go away. I knew that he had only to see Marie to guess my secret. But, more than anything else, I dreaded your meeting him, dreaded your suspicions – and his. But when you did come . . . I hate telling you this . . . I was jealous. You seemed capable of dominating even a man like him, and that I found exasperating. I wonder whether you can understand my state of mind at that time? You see, what nearly drove me demented was the knowledge that you completely controlled my life. I had never felt that quite so acutely before, because it had never been so much in your power before to dispose of my heart, to make or mar my happiness. The more I think about what happened, the more clearly do I see that only anger could have screwed me up to the point of going to his room, as I did . . ."

So utterly was Gisèle's mind occupied with the memory of that now distant drama, so wholly was she in the grip of the Christian passion for self-examination, that she was quite unaware of the figure trembling there beside her, for all the world as though she had received a blow.

"It's only now that I really understand what I felt then. He knew the shameful truth about me . . . I had nothing to lose . . . God had turned away from me. It wasn't for your sake that I resisted him. On the contrary, it was the thought of you that tempted me to indulge in an act of defiance. It wasn't enough for you to influence me through Marie. You wanted to drive all love from my heart, that you might be its undisputed mistress . . ."

"That is not true!"

With a single movement, Lucile de Villeron sprang to her feet. She repeated the words:

"That is not true!"

Taken aback by the violence of her tone, Gisèle tried to touch her hands: but they were snatched away.

"So it was I, only I, who drove you into sin!"

"I never said that!"

"And if I had not been 'inspired' – as you put it – to leave you free, you would have gone back to that man . . . simply and solely to run away from me . . . only my *not* being there saved you! . . . a nice thing, that, for me to know!"

"I never said any such thing, Lucile . . .!"

Madame de Villeron had gone to the far end of the room. She turned now, and came back towards her friend.

"And what about the first time, my girl?" she said with bitter sarcasm: "I suppose you'll say it was all because I was with you, because you wanted to shake yourself free of me . . ."

At the sound of a long-drawn moan from Gisèle she broke off, jarred back to her senses. She covered her face with her hands.

"Darling . . . how could I speak like that to you . . . Oh, my child . . . my child!"

She put her arms about the bowed and broken body on the couch, forced it upright, leaned the tear-stained face against her shoulder, and soothed her as though she had, indeed, been her little daughter. Not now would

K

she probe her conscience: for that she must wait until she was alone. Dear God! what precipices do we skirt unknowingly – like sleep-walkers on a roof!

Gisèle, now half-consoled, and in a humble mood, was begging for forgiveness:

"How *could* you believe that! Why, I owe everything to you, Lucile. Far apart though we were, it was you who saved me – for the second time. From all that you have suffered, *I* have profited . . ."

Madame de Villeron shook her head:

"God had no need of me . . . of my utter wretchedness . . . You did well to remind me of that."

With bitter clarity of vision she looked at the young woman, upright now on the couch, though still trembling.

"Even while I was having those horrible thoughts", Gisèle said, "I still respected you, still revered you . . . But now they are far from me. You are my salvation in this world and the next . . ."

Lucile's lips parted in a strange smile: but it did not touch her eyes.

"Don't be too sure of that" she said: "which of us can be sure that we are saved before our end has come?"

"Alas! that is only too true! Each time I came back I thought it was for good and all . . . How true the words are that you once wrote to me: *There are those for whom each return is as useless as a cry* . . . That was one of the sayings, do you remember, which I included in my collection? – and there's this other one – *Sometimes, evil desires grow most vigorously in the heart that has been ploughed by contrition* – I remember that one too. My heart, Lucile, is like the pendulum of the clock over there on the mantelpiece: it swings up, it swings down: then up again, down again . . ."

"One day it will mount and mount, and there will be no more 'down' . . ."

Madame de Villeron tried hard to find something else to say, but at last relapsed into silence, suddenly grown tired of staying on the heights, conscious of a deadly fatigue. She could have found it in her heart that Gisèle should comfort *her* – though comfort for what, she did not know. The younger woman sighed:

"I have to start my climb from too great a depth: did anyone ever fall so low as I have done?"

Lucile felt too irritated to answer, as she would have liked to do – "almost everybody, my poor dear!" The clock struck the hour in the rain–dark room. Gisèle got up, and put on her hat again before the glass.

"Won't you stay and have dinner with us?"

Mademoiselle de Plailly replied that she *must* catch the 8 p.m. train from the Gare du Nord. She hoped the rain would have stopped before she got back, because there would be no car waiting for her at the station, and she would have to walk the three miles. Her father would be getting impatient. And then, as usual, she began to enumerate in detail all the things she would find waiting to be done. Lucile, not listening, said in a low voice: "so you're really going away?" – and looked round the room which held no meaning for her, as though she had never seen it before. For the first time she was conscious of the hostility lurking in the corners of this rented house. She dreaded the evening that lay ahead, the hurried, silent meal – the prospect of loneliness, the thought of the night to come. "Oh, do, do stay!" she softly moaned... Gisèle stopped what she was doing, and asked:

"What was that you said?"

Madame de Villeron shook her head, and, in reply, muttered a barely audible – "nothing". Then, getting to her feet she went ahead of Gisèle as far as the garden door, in spite of the rain. Gisèle turned her head and smiled at Marie who was flattening her nose against one of the ground floor windows.

"Don't stay here, Lucile: you'll get drenched!"

"When will you come again?"

The other hesitated for a moment. then –

"Listen", she said, "it was because of me that you came to Versailles ... The best thing, I think ... but after what has happened this afternoon, I'm afraid you may take what I'm going to say in bad part, but you won't, will you? . . . God knows I don't want to be parted from you . . . but I do think the best thing you can do is to go back to Dunkirk. I have thought a lot about all this, Lucile . . . I have no right to monopolize you: you belong to others. But you *must* promise to write to me – often, every day if you can . . . and, above all, you must pray for me . . . If I feel myself in danger, I will send for you . . . and *of course* you must bring Marie to me for Christmas."

Lucile de Villeron did not move. She was trying, it seemed, to get a grip on herself. At last she spoke. She thanked God, she said, that her presence was no longer necessary. She would go home in the course of the following week. Then, after a brief embrace, Mademoiselle de Plailly ran through the pouring rain towards the tram-stop. Lucile stood for a long while looking after her, and even after she had vanished, remained standing where she was. She could feel the rain on her face and shoulders. After some considerable while she returned to the house, and once more settled down in her wicker chair, without switching on the light. Marie was quietly playing at trains on the rose-coloured couch. All she could see was a stiff and upright figure sitting near her; but what she heard was a medal clicking against the beads of a rosary.

V

DANIEL TRASIS was sitting at a café opposite the Gare du Nord. He was putting up a pretence of being interested in the conversation of an outside broker. Raymond Courrège had written him a note suggesting that it might be worth while finding out whether "the bloke's got anything to him". But, from the very first words uttered by the stranger – something to do with a deal in Rumanian Bonds – Daniel felt instinctively that what was in the wind was one of those shady operations of which the prudent Raymond always fought shy. All the time that he was nodding agreement with what the broker was saying, his hungry eyes were fixed on the surge and eddy of the crowd which was swarming round the entrance to the station on this August Sunday morning.

Ever since getting back he had been careful not to write to Gisèle, or rather, had been careful not to post the letters which he *had* written. Each evening he fed his hunger on the sheets which the girl had slipped under his door. Over those mad, yet rather too carefully written pages, he dreamed in the warm darkness, safe from all interruption. August in Paris meant an empty building, a silent telephone, a somnolent concierge. In the daytime, active in body but slothful in mind, he occupied the hours with business. Raymond Courrège was rushing back and forth between Deauville and Cabourg, dealing with the orders of dilatory customers who had waited until the season was at its height to begin thinking about buying open tourers. Daniel, meanwhile, made the round of the garages, arranging meetings, and pocketing commissions, part of which he telegraphed to Courrège. But as soon as darkness fell, he went back to that letter, marvelling at the knowledge that he felt no jealousy. He knew so well, he thought, what that young Cadet must have looked like, and dressed him in the features of those many poor young boys whom he had so often comforted in some stinking dug-out on the eve of an attack. He even felt touched at the fate of the unknown youth. No, he did not experience the least twinge of jealousy. There were evenings when he lay sweating on the divan in his room, smoking and day-dreaming, watching the vague shapes of his brooding thoughts take visible form and then dissolve like clouds. He saw Lucile de Villeron picking an injured swallow from the dust, and launching it into the blue. He remembered a schoolfellow, one day at Mass, pointing to some words which he had underlined with his finger-nail, and spluttering with suppressed laughter – *the law of the members* . . . He conjured up a picture of the striped fire-balloons rising into the air above the vineyards of the Gironde on the eve of August 15th, soaring to a great height, and then suddenly bursting into flame. One year the burning debris had set fire to the dry heath, and the rise and fall of the sounding tocsin had roused the village. Gisèle! – he remembered the moonlight on the sheets . . . Then, mad with desire, he would sit down at his table and scribble an imperious summons, knowing full well that he would tear it up when morning came. Against this fear of "rigging" the game there was nothing he could do. Gisèle! innocence proof against the heat of passion: snow that was stronger than the sun.

Something of a quite different kind had left him open to a flood of curious preoccupations. Sister Lodois had recently sent him news – expressed in high falutin language (on behalf of the Ransinangues, who had never learned to write), that Marie Ransinangue had died of consumption at her convent after months of illness . . . She had suffered much, especially in spirit, said the Sister. She had believed that God had abandoned her, had wavered in her faith, and had seen the light once more only a few days before her death. But, at the end, a radiant smile had touched her sleeping face, and had stayed there even after life had flown. She had been buried before corruption had had time to touch her body.

At first, when the news came, Daniel had shrugged.

But, later, he had read the letter through again. It brought vividly back into his mind that rutted road at Bourrideys (when he was sixteen it had meant a way of escape from Uncle Louprat), and the dark, tree-encumbered house. It had been while he had been lying beside Marie Ransinangue at the edge of a field of maize, that he had first been afflicted by this strange craving of his for innocence…

And now here he was in a Paris café, in company with a talkative broker who was putting questions to him, and trying to get authority from him for what he had been doing. Daniel said little, merely expressing, with vague movements of his hands and head, a general agreement with the suggestions put forward by his companion. His attention was held by the milling crowd round the Gare du Nord on this Sunday morning. It was as though he were expecting Gisèle de Plailly to emerge suddenly from its midst. For a moment he half believed that the very violence of his longing would bring her like a female Lazarus through those tomb-like doors. He called to her in thought, evoked her presence with a fierce authority, while he arranged with the broker the time and place of their next meeting. At last he was alone, with nothing to distract him from those yawning exits through which the suburban crowd was spilling out on to the pavement. He struck his forehead with his clenched left hand. "Fool! fool!" he said aloud. Courrège had announced his own imminent return. Between now and then he must get matters settled. What was this poison which, ever since Argelès, had clouded his vision of the world? He suddenly felt ashamed of the hazy imaginings with which, for some days now, he had been all too willingly indulging himself. One doesn't realize how much rubbish can be left by receding childhood on the beaches of consciousness – so much false sentiment, so much of what Courrège called "fudge". "I've had about enough!" he growled to himself, and pushing his hat to the back of his head, called for pen and paper. In a few words of mingled arrogance and tenderness, he wrote to Gisèle, telling her to join him. This brief letter he signed with his Christian name. Only when it was finished did he remember that she would not get it till the next morning. It was most unlikely that there were more than two Sunday deliveries in her village. How long would he have to drag on before her answer came? He decided that he could not face even the short delay involved. He feared the instability of his feelings, and wanted to take advantage of what might be only a fleeting mood. His eyes were still upon those yawning doors which led into that not so distant land where Gisèle de Plailly lived. Why, it suddenly occurred to him, should he not make the trip in person? He could take a train and be with her this very day! Under the influence of that new certainty he grew less agitated. He would carry her off with him. Where should they go? Only yesterday he had received from the Ransinangues the money due to him from the sale of his resin. The past month had brought him a number profitable deals. He had never felt so rich. He thought of the poor fallen creature now an exile from her own people. He would begin by intoxicating her with luxury. At this season of the year there was no lack of smart hotels and gay crowds to choose from. "Biarritz" – he thought – "I'll send a wire to the Carlton." But even while he heard in imagination an orchestra playing in a lounge with great bays opening on glazed segments of sky and sea, filled with women all bare backs and pearl necklaces, he decided that he could not picture her in such surroundings. The image he retained of her was of someone with dusty boots and blouses which she never changed even when they went their evening walks. He saw her hatless, with grass stains on her piqué skirt from the banks beside the chattering waterfall. No, she was not like other women . . . even in surrender there had been in her a strange solemnity. Never once had she spoken of that luxury for which almost every other woman of his acquaintance would have given her eyes, and certainly would have willingly sold herself. He doubted whether the thought of it had ever entered her mind. He forgot her prattle, the ease with which she gave herself, her insatiable craving for caresses, and found himself thinking only of a unique individual who, even when possessed, surrendered nothing of her mystery or her charm. Moved by the same impulse which, one hot afternoon at Argelès, had sent him hot-foot to her room, he crossed the open space before the station at a run. At the booking-office he asked for a ticket to Louvres . . .

He found somebody to direct him to the village, and walked on, not recognizing the country as she had des-cribed it to him – the stinking miles of chemical manure, the flocks of crows scarcely blacker than the lowering sky, the debris of agricultural implements showing above the surface of the mud like the skeletons of a vanished species. The season had not yet come when beetroot pulp would lie rotting in the silos. This summer's day knew nothing of such things. Across the plain, right up to the slopes of Montmélian, stacked bare poles gave the im-pression of an enormous camp stretching as far as the eye could reach. There was nothing to break the silence ex-cept the whirr of a mechanical reaper and the shrilling of a skylark far above his head. As the bird was attracted by the sun, so was he by her village, and covered the three miles at a great pace, and hatless. So used was he to the blazing sky above his native Landes that the veiled sun-light of the Valois country caused him not the least dis-comfort.

Would he see Gisèle? He had made no plans. As he walked through the village, the bells were ringing for Mass. But the unkempt women on their doorsteps, and the children playing in the street, just as she had described them, seemed unaware that it was Sunday. He caught the glint of zinc far back in a gloomy ground floor interior where bare-headed men stood clustered round a bar, as about the altar of some alien faith to be celebrated in bouts of copious drinking. He went into the church, and passed at once from sunshine to a twilit world peopled only by a few old women and children. The three church-going families of the place were duly ranged upon their benches. In the half-empty nave a group of young girls was gathered round a harmonium. Perched on a high stool at the keyboard, and visible above the cluster of singing faces, sat Gisèle de Plailly. Like some Virgin of the Assumption she dominated the kneeling Children of Mary. She was leaning slightly forward, her hair touched by a beam of sunlight, and was swaying slightly, as though not quite sure that the Angels would bear her up. At the moment of the Consecration she slid from her seat and became merged in the kneeling singers. When the Host was raised she bent low in deep abasement, then rose again to accompany the few shrill voices of her choir:

Le voici l'agneau si doux . . .

The little threadbare chant echoed forlornly in the

spaces of this church which was so very much too large
for it. The last verse died into silence. From the world
outside came the laughing voices of boys, and the neigh-
ing of a horse which, as soon as the final blessing had
been given, would carry the priest back to his distant
parish. Gisèle, as though suspended midway between
Heaven and the muddy earth, sat swaying above the tiny
group of girls at prayer. "If she could see me," thought
Daniel, "she would come running." Was it pain or happiness he felt? He could have found no words in which
to describe the sharpness of his anguish, his dread lest he
might be interrupting a miracle. At the tinkle of the
Sacring Bell she knelt again and, quite alone, approached
the altar rail. When she returned to her seat, Daniel hid
himself. But even if he had not done so she would not
have seen him, being utterly turned in upon herself,
moving slowly and as though weighed down under a
load of bliss, so that she could not rise, but must stay
upon the earth, cast down, and lost – and saved.

He moved a little way from the shadow. Why should
he hide any longer? Never again would Gisèle have eyes
for the things of this world. Because he knew that he was
no longer an object of fear, he was conscious of an angry
surge of jealousy. He looked about him at the empty and
neglected church, observed attentively the final gestures,
the last whispering of the hurried priest. Unconsidered

and despised though these ancient rites might be by the village schoolmaster and the local waggoners, it was they, and what they represented that had the power to cleanse the heart and body of Gisèle de Plailly, fall though she might, not once but many times, unto seventy times seven, giving her back unceasingly the sanctity of innocence . . . Daniel moved out into the nave. "She has only to turn her head and she will see me . . ." Ashamed, and without joy, he forced himself to keep alive this vain bravado. Should he lie in wait for her at the door? She would almost certainly be the last to leave, after – what had it been called at school? – after making her Act of Thanksgiving. Péloueyre had beaten all records with his Acts of Thanksgiving, and had invariably brought up the rear . . . "It is too soon after the Communion . . . I should have no success, she would still be under the influence of . . ." – he dared not speak the Name. Only after several hours had passed would Gisèle emerge from her spellbound state.

The little group of worshippers was crowding round the holy water stoup at the door. As he had foreseen, the girl was left alone. An altar-boy was going round extinguishing the candles, and his iron shod boots rang on the flags. To Daniel it seemed that the beating of his heart made inaudible the shouts and laughter from outside the church. He saw Gisèle upon her knees, her mind centred upon some inner truth, creating behind her joined hands that darkness in which the faithful can hear and see their Saviour. He made one last effort to rid himself of compassion, of a most strange distress shot through with hope . . . Staring at his watch, he said to himself: "If in three minutes she does not get up, I will bother about her no longer." Second by second he followed the movement of the hand . . . But from the night which she had built about herself, Gisèle de Plailly did not return.

Daniel leaned above the ancient and abandoned font, and gazed into those depths from which the hearts and bodies of young women lost could still emerge, having put on a new glory . . . "If only she doesn't see me . . ." He backed away with bated breath, reached the door, dipped his finger in the Water, signed his forehead, breast and shoulders, and walked away.